THE CASE OF THE FOUR FLYING FINGERS

By the Same Author

The Case of the Four Flying Fingers

A McGurk Mystery

BY E. W. HILDICK
ILLUSTRATED BY LISL WEIL

MACMILLAN PUBLISHING CO., INC.
New York

Macmillan Publishing Co., Inc.
866 Third Avenue, New York, N.Y. 10022
Collier Macmillan Canada, Ltd.
Printed in the United States of America

10 9 8 7 6 5 4 3 2

LIBRARY OF CONGRESS CATALOGING IN PUBLICATION DATA
Hildick, E. W. (Edmund Wallace), date.
The case of the four flying fingers.
(A McGurk mystery)
SUMMARY: While unwittingly helping a
master burglar, a group of children runs afoul
of the McGurk Detective Organization.
[1. Mystery and detective stories]   I. Weil, Lisl.
II. Title. III. Series.
PZ7.H5463Casf   [Fic]   81-2517
ISBN 0-02-743880-5   AACR2

Contents

1 McGurk Decides to Advertise

CRASH! BAM! WHIZZ! CLATTER!

The special meeting of the McGurk Organization sure started off with a bang *that* morning!

It was the Thursday before the Easter weekend and the first day of the school spring vacation. McGurk had just begun to tell us what was on his mind.

"This time last year we were about to tackle one of our trickiest cases." He tapped the box of files on the table—the one labeled MYSTERIES SOLVED "The Great Rabbit Rip-off. Remember?"

We nodded. At least I, Joey Rockaway, nodded, and so did Wanda Grieg and Willie Sandowsky. But Brains Bellingham was shaking his bristly blond

1

head and blinking critically behind his big glasses.

"Correction, McGurk. *You* were about to tackle that one. You and the others. I was not a member of the Organization at that time. Although, come to think of it, I *was* able to give you information that helped you solve—"

"Whatever!" said McGurk, waving Brains down. "The point is this. Last year we had a big juicy case to work on. This time all we have is a request from Mrs. Kranz to keep an eye on her house while she's away for the weekend."

He paused in his rocking in the old chair at the head of the table. He leaned forward. His green eyes gleamed above his freckles. His red hair flared in a shaft of sunlight.

"So I say we make the best of it," he went on. "I say we *build* on it. And—"

And that's when we heard the crash. An almighty crash. Just as if McGurk really had started to build something out in his yard and someone had come along and kicked it over.

We ran out of the basement door and up the steps into the yard.

We saw at once what had happened. Willie, who was in the lead, nearly fell over the garbage can. It was lying there on its side, still rolling gently.

That had been the *CRASH!* and the *BAM!*

Wanda stooped to pick up the lid. It had been sent flying and was sticking in the lower branches of a bush.

That must have been the *WHIZZ!*

As for the *CLATTER!*—McGurk, Brains, and I were making it happen again, as we ran through the scattered junk, stumbling into empty jars and cans that had spilled from the burst garbage bags.

We were heading for the street, toward the sounds of shouts and cries and gasps and giggles.

"Hey, what d'ya think you're doing?!" yelled McGurk, skidding on a slice of fatty ham that had spilled onto the driveway with the rest of the goo.

He was addressing four little kids—all boys—age

about seven or eight. They were already darting into another driveway, two doors away.

"They're playing Cowboys and Indians from the look of it," said Brains.

Sure enough, one of the kids had a big white feather stuck through a red sweatband around his forehead. Another had a battered old hat on his head-stetson type and several sizes too big for him. All of them were either pretending to wave tomahawks or shoot with their fingers as they ran in and out of the shrubs lining the driveway.

"*BAM!* Gotcha!"

"Ya missed!"

"Look out, Sam!"

"I'll scalp ya!"

Even as we watched, the one with the feather ran in back of the garbage can, while the hat kid dove after him. And:

CRASH! BAM! CLATTER!

Another garbage can bit the dust. Then the kids were on their way, yelling and whooping and laughing and screaming.

"Children!" said Brains (who's only ten himself!). "All wrapped up in their game. I bet they don't even know what a mess they've been making."

"They'd be all wrapped up in some of this goo if

I got my hands on them!" I said grimly, trying to scrape off a hunk of peanut butter from the side of one of my new brown loafers.

"Forget them!" growled McGurk. "Give me a hand cleaning up the mess before my mother blames *us* for it!"

It took us about five minutes to get everything back in the can. It might even have taken twice as long, what with Wanda grumbling about not wanting to get grease on her new jeans, and me busily trying to get grease out of the fancy punched pattern holes in my loafers, and Willie sniffing at the empty cans and jars and saying what had been in them, and Brains going on about the curious scientific fact that spilled garbage always seems to take up more space when you try to put it back.

But McGurk cut through it all by saying, "Come

on, come on! We have a business to run and I was just going to make a very important announcement."

So it wasn't long before we were trooping back into the basement, through the door with the notice that read:

HEADQUARTERS

KEEP OUT

THE MCGURK ORGANIZATION

❋   ❋   ❋   ❋   ❋

PRIVATE INVESTIGATIONS

MYSTERIES SOLVED

PERSONS PROTECTED

MISSING PERSONS FOUND

MONSTERS EXORCISED

SPIES UNMASKED

—not forgetting the extra bit recently tacked on, on a separate strip of paper, in McGurk's flowery printing:

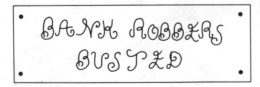

That notice was like a scroll of honor—a capsule history of all our greatest triumphs—and the sight of it put us all in an eagerly receptive mood as we sat around the table.

"Now then," said McGurk, settling back and rocking gently, "where was I?"

"Building on something," said Brains.

"Yes, this dumb house-minding job," said Wanda.

"You said we were to make the best of it," said Willie.

"*Build* on it, you said," I muttered, taking another glance at my loafers.

"Oh—yeah!" McGurk hunched forward again. "Right, men! O.K. . . . So it isn't the most exciting job in the world, keeping an eye on someone's house while they're away. And maybe nothing will happen—"

"I should hope *not!*" said Wanda. "We don't want Mrs. Kranz to be burglarized just to make life exciting for *you,* McGurk!"

"But if we went in for it in a big way," said McGurk, ignoring her, "if we got ten, maybe twenty people to hire us, the chances are we *will* be able to catch someone breaking and entering."

Even Wanda began to look interested now. Somehow it didn't seem so bad, put that way.

Brains pushed his glasses further up his nose.

"Yes" he said. "Quite correct, McGurk. The Law

of Averages. And there *has* been an increase in break-ins lately. Over on the north side of town. I was reading about it just yesterday."

"But how do we get that many people to hire us, McGurk?" said Wanda. "I haven't noticed any new clients beating a path to this door lately."

"By advertising," said McGurk. "*That's* how!" I straightened up from my fiftieth gloomy inspection of the grease-stained loafer. This sounded interesting.

"Advertising?"

"Yes, Joey. Leaflets mainly. It's a bit late. The weekend's nearly here. But if we work fast we can still let a whole lot of people know about the services we can offer."

"*Services?*" I said. "Plural? You mean doing *more* than just keeping an eye on property?"

"*Much* more!" said McGurk. "Listen. . . ."

This time we all hunched forward with him.

He'd gotten us hooked now, all right. As usual. I mean, no one—but *no* one—can lick McGurk at transforming what looks like a dull job into something rich and glittering and exciting. *Midas* McGurk he should have been called, instead of Jack.

But—Jack or Midas—even he didn't know just *how* exciting this case was going to be.

HAVE YOUR HOME
WATCHED·BY·EXPERTS

THE McGURK ORGANIZATION'S
SERVICES ARE UNIQUE!

2 The Leaflet

"What we have to do," said McGurk, "is break the job down into—"

"Oh, come on, McGurk!" said Wanda. "First you say *build* on it. Then you say *break it down*. Make up your mind!"

Wanda is like that. Quick to lose patience with McGurk. Always ready to pounce on him when she thinks he might be conning us. Sometimes she's right. *Then* when she pounces, he snaps back in self-defense.

But when he really does have a good idea, he doesn't seem to hear her protests and criticisms. He simply continues outlining his plans—eyes gleaming.

He did that now.

"We break the task down into separate things. Separate skills. *Special* skills. Like we put at the top of the leaflet: HAVE YOUR HOME WATCHED BY EXPERTS. That's the *general* idea. O.K.?"

He was looking at me. I mean, I'm the Organization's word expert and expert typist. I was going to be the one who finally licked the leaflet into shape.

"Sure," I said. "That's a pretty good start. Go on."

"Then we put something like: REGULAR PATROL GUARANTEED. O.K.?"

I nodded. "That's still only general, though. Where do the *special* skills come in?

He grinned.

"That's just what people reading the leaflet will be wondering. So then we mention how we'll regularly try all doors—back, side, or front—to make sure they're properly secure. The same for all windows."

"There's nothing very expert about *that*," said Wanda.

"No," said McGurk. "But now we get down to the nitty-gritty. The part that proves the McGurk Organization's services are—uh—united?" He glanced at me. "No? So what *is* the word that means *one of a kind*?"

"*Unique*," I said. "The McGurk Organization's services are *unique*."

"Right!" he said, slapping the table. "Like we put next: *Smoke sniffed out by the most unique and sensitive nose in the business.*"

He smiled proudly at Willie. The most unique and sensitive nose in the business started to redden. Willie was blushing.

"Gee! Well! Yeah! But—*smoke*, Mr. McGurk?"

"Sure, Willie! Folks who go on vacation aren't just worried about burglars. They worry about fires, too. And whether those fires'll be spotted in time."

"There *are* smoke-detecting devices," said Brains. "Linked with local firehouses. Giving early warning that way."

"Sure" said McGurk. "Costing thousands of dollars. But none of them come as cheap as Willie's nose here. Or as sensitive. That's why folks are gonna be crazy about *our* service."

Brains looked a bit put down. McGurk cheered him up immediately.

"But there *are* other scientific things. Things that aren't as expensive as electronic smoke-warning systems and burglar alarms. And that's where *you* come in Brains."

Brains blinked rapidly, thoughtfully.

"Well, sure. I—I guess I could give expert *advice* on things like that. And—yes! I could fix a very cheap automatic light system for anyone who wanted it. One that switches itself on when it gets dark and clicks off again when it's daylight."

"Great!" said McGurk. He turned to Wanda. "Now do you see what I'm getting at?"

She nodded. Two pink spots on her cheeks showed she was getting as enthusiastic as the rest of us.

"As tree-climbing expert and specialist in bushes and all growing things," she began, "I—"

"Yeah!" said Willie. "You can water the plants!"

He meant it seriously, carried away by his own enthusiasm.

It was hard to tell which of them looked more scornful: Wanda or McGurk.

"I can pinpoint the trees and bushes which a burglar would find most useful to *lurk* and *loiter* in," Wanda said firmly. "And I can very quickly climb any suspect trees and search them, just to make sure".

"Atta girl, Officer Grieg!" said McGurk. "That's exactly what I had in mind. As for you, Joey—"

"Yeah," I said, a bit doubtfully. "I guess there isn't much need for a word expert on a house security patrol. But I *could* keep my eyes open for things like newspapers and mail. You know. Make sure there's nothing like that lying around exposed and giving away the fact that a house is unoccupied."

"Good thinking, Officer Rockaway," said McGurk. "But even more important than that is writing out, and typing out, and making copies of the leaflets that are going to get us our House Patrol customers. O.K.?"

"O.K.!" I said, already starting to scribble away at the first rough copy.

And here is the final typed version, which we then ran off on our copying machine, so that at the end of the morning we had over 100 leaflets to distribute:

```
            HAVE YOUR HOME WATCHED
                 BY EXPERTS
         Enjoy your vacation with complete
                  peace of mind.

            THE McGURK ORGANIZATION
                  offers you:
         Guaranteed regular patrols.
         All doors and first-floor windows
         checked 3 times a day.

         ALSO THE FOLLOWING EXPERT SERVICES:
          Smoke-sniffing by the most sensitive human
         apparatus (Officer W. Sandowsky's unique nose).
          Free technical advice from our resident
         science expert (Officer G. Bellingham).

          Inexpensive automatic light systems fixed
         to order.
          Trees and bushes regularly (and thoroughly)
         searched for lurkers and loiterers by
         Officer W. Grieg.
                                      (over)
```

Then, on the other side, there was this:

```
    Uncollected mail, leaflets, newspapers,
    etc. quickly spotted and put out of sight
    by Officer J. Rockaway.

    PLUS:
    Constant supervision by Jack P. McGurk
    (Head of Organization) whose uncanny
    eye for Suspicious characters in the
    neighborhood will ensure that most of
    them don't even get to first base.

    Fee: 50¢ per household per day.

    (NOTE: The Organization regrets that due to
    terrific demand for our expert services, we
    cannot undertake non-security chores like
    watering plants or feeding pets.)
```

Well, as anyone who knows much about the Organization will have noticed, the wording wasn't entirely my own. Wanda had to insist on that "and thoroughly" bit—even though I pointed out that it made it look as if we other experts might do *our* jobs sloppily. And, of course, McGurk had to keep putting *his* trimmings in.

But on the whole I was very proud of those leaflets. We all were.

"We'll probably have to hire extra staff for the patrols," said Wanda.

"Yes—swear in some deputies," I said.

"No way!" said McGurk. "We keep this exclusive. We've got standards to maintain."

He needn't have worried.

We were going to be kept busy, sure enough. And, sure enough, we were going to be kept busy patrolling and protecting vacated houses.

But the business was going to come through a very different channel than those leaflets.

"The Galloping
3 Garbage Gang"

McGurk very quickly worked out a plan for distributing those leaflets.

"We start right after lunch," he said. "We don't deliver them to our own houses, of course. And we don't deliver them to houses where they've already gone away for the weekend."

"No," said Brains. "And there's no point in delivering them to houses where we know for a fact that they're *not* going away. Like my Aunt Christine, next door."

"Right!" said McGurk. "But speaking of next door, we *do* start delivering close to Headquarters here and work our way gradually around and out."

"Why?" said Willie.

"Because *that* way," said McGurk, "when all the orders start pouring in, we can save time on patrol by not having so far to go."

That guy was *brimming* with confidence!

This made him all the more impatient after lunch, when Wanda and Brains didn't show until 1:40—ten minutes late.

They both arrived together, looking very annoyed, very hot, and very messy.

I noticed that last thing right away, I mean, it wasn't like Brains to have clots of fried egg clinging to the sleeve of his sweater. Nor was it like Wanda to have glittering tomato seeds and pieces of corn sticking in her long blond hair.

McGurk didn't seem to see these things. All he did was glare at his watch, then at the pile of leaflets, and then at the latecomers.

"What kept you?" he growled.

"Those dumb kids!" said Wanda, glaring back.

"Same here!" said Brains, suddenly wrinkling his nose in disgust as he looked at *his* watch and saw the bits of egg nestling above it. "There ought to be a law!"

"*What* dumb kids?" said McGurk.

"The Cowboys and Indians kids!" said Wanda,

trying to comb some of the mess out of her hair with her fingertips.

"The *garbage* kids!" snarled Brains.

McGurk rolled his eyes angrily.

"You mean you've been wasting Organization time playing with little kids?"

"No! *Not* playing! Cleaning up after them!" snapped Brains. "They weren't even anywhere around."

"I wish they *had* been," grumbled Wanda. "Boy do I wish they had been!"

Having removed the last of the egg from his sleeve, Brains calmed down.

"It looks as if they've developed a taste for knocking over garbage cans," he said thoughtfully.

"All along our street," said Wanda.

"And ours," said Brains. "Seems like they found it more fun than Cowboys and Indians. They're doing it on purpose now."

Wanda sighed. She'd given up on her hair. She tossed it back over her shoulders and said:

"If only garbage pick-up hadn't been switched from Thursday to Tuesday morning! The cans would have been almost empty and it wouldn't have taken to long to clean things up."

"So *long?*" howled McGurk. *"Ten minutes?* Ten

whole minutes of the Organization's valuable time just to scrape up some old garbage?"

Wanda scowled at him.

"It took five of us all of five minutes to scrape up *yours*, this morning, McGurk. Remember? And I had to do ours by myself."

"So did I," said Brains. But he was still looking thoughtful. "And—hey—listen, McGurk. Why don't we make *this* our new case? Obviously those kids are doing it on purpose now. With *intent*. That makes it sheer vandalism—a crime we haven't dealt much with before."

"Hey, yes!" said Wanda. Now she was looking less angry—more interested in getting even. "Littering the streets. I mean, O.K.—so maybe it isn't a federal offense. But Brains is right. It *is* a real crime. Better than working on a crime that might never be committed at all, like this house watching."

McGurk suddenly grinned, in a sneery sort of way.

"You know your trouble—both of you? You're just sore. Sure—it *is* a crime. But *what* a crime! Just kid stuff. Just four little dumb kids!"

I was all set to agree with McGurk. I mean, I'd *slaved away* at those leaflets. I didn't want to abandon them now. So I sneered, too.

"Yes!" I said to Wanda and Brains. "You'll have us tracking down little dogs for messing up the sidewalk next!"

Willie laughed.

"Yeah! The Case of the Mutts' Mistakes!"

Even Brains and Wanda had to smile. After all, it isn't every day that Willie comes up with a joke as fast as that.

McGurk wasn't going to be outdone, though—either at sneering or joking.

"And what would you have Joey call *this* one for the records? The Case of the Galloping Garbage Gang? . . . Come on. We're wasting time."

Faced with such a barrage of jeers and sneers, Wanda and Brains gave in, and soon we were on our way delivering the leaflets.

Well, we stuck exactly to McGurk's plan. We covered the near neighborhood systematically. We left out our own houses, the houses where the people had already gone away, and the houses where we knew for a fact that they weren't going away.

And we did this in spite of the sneers and jeers directed at *all* of us by smart alecks like Burt Rafferty.

"Hey, look!" he cried, when he saw us shoving our leaflets under the doors. "The McJerk Organization can't get a case, so they're going around delivering free coupons from the supermarket!"

21

Sandra Ennis even accused *us* of littering the neighborhood.

But none of this deterred McGurk—not even when we came across some more spilled garbage cans and Wanda and Brains started fussing about the four little kids again. In fact the only thing that slowed him down at all was his own pride. He was so pleased with the leaflets that he must have lovingly read the bit about his "uncanny eye for suspicious characters" at least fifty times.

"That'll grab 'em!" he kept saying.

And:

"You'll see! I bet there's a line forming outside our Headquarters already!"

And:

"Maybe we should have quoted 75 cents a day."

Hah! if we'd quoted 75 *dollars* a day for our expert services, the result couldn't have been more disappointing.

Because there was no line outside our HQ when we got back. There was not even a *single* customer waiting to sign us up.

No one came hammering at our door during the rest of the afternoon or evening, either.

No. The only message we did get was from the

customer we'd had already, before all that sweating and toiling over the leaflets.

It was Mrs. Kranz on the McGurks' phone.

"Don't forget I leave early in the morning," she reminded McGurk, when he answered. "And I do hope these leaflets won't bring you in so much work you won't be able to keep a regular watch on *my* house."

"Don't worry, Mrs. Kranz," said our leader. "We *are* expecting a big—uh—surge of interest tonight, when folks have had time to think about it. But you'll still be at the top of our list!"

Reassuring Mrs. Kranz seemed to hearten *him*, too. It often happens like that with McGurk. I mean that guy really *believes* his own sales pitches.

Anyway, when he'd hung up, he turned to us with the old glow on his face.

"O.K., men! Early to bed tonight. Tomorrow it looks like we'll have a big work load on our hands!"

4 More Garbage

McGurk was 50 percent right in what he'd said to Mrs. Kranz. Come Friday morning she was definitely at the top of the list. She could hardly have been anyplace else. She was the only customer *on* the list.

But as for the "big surge of interest"—no. Not unless you counted the surge of interest in paper airplanes—made out of our leaflets. Or the surge of interest shown by some of the smart alecks in murdering the English language.

For example, here's what we saw nailed to Burt Rafferty's front gatepost. Our leaflet with the heading changed to:

```
┌─────────────────────────────────────────┐
│                    RECK                   │
│      HAVE YOUR HOME W̶A̶T̶C̶H̶ED             │
│            BY EXPERTS                      │
```

McGurk tore it down in disgust.

Sandra Ennis had been at work, too. She'd done a nasty little number on some of the expert services. She'd changed Willie's to:

```
        signalling
  Smoke-s̶n̶i̶f̶f̶i̶n̶g̶ b̶y̶ the most sensitive.human
                          unicorn
  apparatus (Officer W. Sandowsky's u̶n̶i̶q̶u̶e̶ nose).
```

Brains's light system service had been changed to:

```
  Inexpensive automatic light systems fixed
  to o̶r̶d̶e̶r̶. blow every fuse in the house.
```

So it wasn't just McGurk but all of us who were feeling pretty ruffled by the time we reached Mrs. Kranz's house. And at first this feeling wasn't helped by what we saw in the driveway.

Wanda spotted it first.

"Oh, *no!*" she groaned.

She had just put her foot in a large hunk of discarded butter. It must have slithered farther than the rest of the garbage: the old cans and bottles and cartons strewn along the driveway. The garbage can itself was lying empty, on its side, up by the garage.

As I shooed away a couple of cats from the remains of a pot roast, Brains said:

"Looks like those kids were *here* yesterday, too!"

But all at once McGurk was looking serious. Not angry-serious. But definitely thoughtful.

"No, Officer Bellingham," he murmured. "Not yesterday. Definitely *today*, this morning. Since 8:30."

"Huh?" said Willie. "How d'you know *that*, Mc-Gurk?"

"Because," said McGurk, gingerly stirring an empty fried chicken bucket with his foot, "Mrs. Kranz didn't leave until that time. And she wouldn't have gone with all this garbage splattered about. No, men. . . . Those kids must still be at it today."

Wanda snorted.

"Big deal!" she said. "Great detective work!"

Brains wasn't so scornful.

"Maybe we ought to make it a case after all," he said.

Now it was McGurk's turn to be scornful. But in a gentle, still thoughtful way.

"Still dying to tackle The Case of the Galloping Garbage Gang, huh, Brains?" He shook his head. "No, men. We may only have one customer so far —but, by Sherlock, we're gonna do that job right!"

He clapped his hands.

"And first," he declared, "we set to work cleaning this mess up."

Well Wanda nearly flipped at that. I guess that in the last twenty-four hours she'd had enough garbage stuck to her person to last a lifetime.

She glared at McGurk. She'd been the one to tear down the mangled leaflet from the Ennis gatepost. Now she pulled it out of her pocket and stabbed a finger at an item near the bottom.

"Come on, McGurk! How about this part *here*— *'cannot undertake non-security chores like watering plants or feeding pets'*? . . . Doesn't cleaning up garbage rate as a non-security chore, too?"

McGurk looked very smug then. That obnoxious know-it-all smile began to spread over his face.

"No, it does *not*, Officer Grieg! Cleaning up garbage rates as *top* security."

"What? Security from *cats*?" snapped Wanda.

McGurk ignored her. He addressed us all.

"Because what did my great detective brain figure the moment I saw this mess? I'll tell you. It figured that Mrs. Kranz must have left the house before it happened, otherwise she'd have cleaned it up herself."

He paused. He smirked. He swelled out his chest.

"And if a great detective brain can figure that, men—so can a great *burglar* brain!"

"Hey, yeah!" said Willie, full of awe.

Brains, too, was looking respectful.

"It advertises the fact that the people are away from home, right, McGurk?"

Even Wanda was impressed. Without any further complaint, she pitched in with the rest of us, as we started to clean up the mess. It made us feel we really were being useful at last in our anticrime patrol.

McGurk himself was so delighted that he looked only *slightly* disappointed when we went on to make our expert checks and found all doors and windows secure, no wisps of smoke coming through ventilators, no lurkers or loiterers in the trees and bushes, and no suspicious characters for McGurk's uncanny eye to spot, out in the street nearby.

He rubbed his hands.

"When Mrs. Kranz comes back on Tuesday she'll

be so pleased, she'll spread it around how good we are. That'll bring in the customers for later vacation periods. Word of mouth. Better than your old leaflets, Joey!"

I *ask* you! *My* old leaflets! As if they'd been *my* idea!

And anyway—what about his "great detective brain?" How come it didn't spot, right then and there, just *how* great and cunning the "burglar brain" in this case really was?

I mean, all the clues and pointers and signs were there already, if only we'd thought about it.

Weren't they?

5 "Burglary!"

It was Wanda who brought the news that finally
alerted McGurk to what was going on.

She arrived breathless at our Headquarters on
Saturday morning, but before she could say anything McGurk was bawling her out.

"Late again, Officer Grieg! We were supposed to
start our patrol fifteen minutes ago! How will you
feel if we find out that Mrs. Kranz's house has been
broken into *during* those fifteen minutes?"

"How will you feel, McGurk," said Wanda, struggling to get back her breath, "when I tell you . . .
huh! . . . that there's been a . . . a real, live, *definite*
burglary in the neighborhood? Huh?"

The glower faded from McGurk's face. An uncertain ripple crossed his forehead. The freckles twitched.

"Is this some kind of joke?"

"Are you some kind of jerk?" Wanda flashed back. "That you can't recognize the truth when you hear it?"

"Uh—sit down, Wanda," said McGurk, politely, but with a kind of bottled-up eagerness. (He isn't a guy for wasting time trading insults when his interest has been caught.) "We believe you." He glared at the rest of us. "At least *I* believe you. . . . Now. About this burglary. Where? Who?"

I was beginning to wonder what had happened to his concern for Mrs. Kranz's house. The way he settled back in his chair made it very clear to me that he was prepared to let that fifteen-minute delay run into fifteen *hours* if necessary.

Then Wanda's next words made *me* forget about the Kranz house, too.

"Mrs. Berg's, that's where. The police are there now. Ray Williams lives next door to her and he told me and he should know. That's why I'm late. I thought you might like to know the details. Maybe I was wrong. Maybe I should have said, 'Sorry, Ray. No time to talk with you. Mustn't be late. McGurk would—' "

"All right, all right!" McGurk swallowed down his annoyance. He even managed a shaky smile. "You did good, Officer Grieg. So now do even better and tell us the details."

"Well, for starters, it was no joke. *I* know when people are telling the truth and Ray *was*—"

"Sure," said McGurk. "I'll buy that. Ray Williams is a friend of ours. Didn't we save his cat from being condemned to death that time? He wouldn't try to pull any smart alecky trick. . . . Go on. What did he tell you?"

"Well, just that Mrs. Berg got back home last night and found the house broken into. She'd been visiting with her oldest daughter, who's just had a baby, and she was coming back to prepare the house for her son Tommy and his family, who're coming to spend the weekend with her—"

"Not *that* kind of detail!" said McGurk—and this time I shared his impatience. We all knew Mrs. Berg. She's a widow with six grown-up sons and daughters. She's always either visiting one of them or having them visit her. Wanda could have gone on for hours about the lady's comings and goings, if McGurk had let her.

"What was missing? Did she surprise any intruders? Was she attacked? Is she seriously injured? Might it turn into a *murder* case?"

Wanda was shaking her head.

"No. She's O.K. I—I think. I mean I don't think anybody was there when she got home. It was late. Ray didn't know what had been stolen. Except— oh, yes—a TV set. I'm only telling you what he told *me.*"

"Huh!" McGurk grunted. "Fifteen minutes to find out a few crummy details like *that!* Remind me to run an interrogation exercise when we have time, Joey. Meanwhile"—he slapped the table and stood up—"let's visit the scene of the crime. Let's interrogate the lady herself."

"But—"

I guess Wanda was going to remind him that the police were already there, doing exactly that.

But McGurk was on his way, up the steps into the yard.

He didn't slow down until he caught sight of the patrol car outside Mrs. Berg's house. And even then it didn't deter him.

"Oh, hi there, Officer Morelli!" he sang out, as the

front door of the house opened and a cop stepped out, tucking away his notebook.

The way McGurk had greeted the patrolman, anyone would think they were lifelong buddies, bowling friends, friends who went on long fishing trips together. Not so. If it had been Patrolman Cassidy, yes. He *is* a friend of ours. But the McGurk Organization had been up against Officer Morelli before—and to say that he could take us or leave us is putting it mildly.

"Outa the way!" he snapped.

McGurk was quick to obey. Good thing too. If he hadn't he'd have been in real danger of being trampled by size-13 boots.

"Don't worry, sir," said McGurk, still polite, still oozing friendship, "we'll give you all the assistance we can. We won't smudge any fingerprints or destroy any evidence. And anything we come up with we'll . . . pass . . . right on . . . to . . . you . . ."

McGurk trailed off. The only response to his generous offer had been the slam of the patrol car door and the gunning of the engine. He shrugged.

"Well, at least he didn't warn us off, men!" he said brightly. Then he turned to the front door and said even more brightly: "Hi, Mrs. Berg! Glad to see they didn't hurt you!"

Mrs. Berg—a plump lady with a smooth pink face —looked puzzled.

"Well, he wasn't the politest policeman I've met. But he didn't *attack* me."

"No, not *him*, ma'am. The intruders. The burglars."

"Oh"—Mrs. Berg gave a little shudder, as if the thought had just occurred to her—"*them!* Oh my, no! They weren't here when I got back. Thank goodness!"

"And when *was* that, ma'am?" McGurk flicked his fingers at me—his usual signal when he wants me to make notes. (I already was, of course.) "The exact time, please."

"Good heavens!" Mrs. Berg was still looking a bit stunned. "You know, I must only have missed them by about twenty minutes. If *that!* Oh—oh dear!"

"Ma'am?"

"Yes. Because I got home just after 11:30. And Mrs. Williams saw the bedroom light go on and off just after eleven. They must have been here *then!*"

"Eleven, huh? Was she sure about that?"

"Mrs. Williams? Yes. She told me she remarked on it to Mr. Williams. 'Mrs. Berg must be back already,' she told him."

"It's a pity Mrs. Williams didn't *call* Mrs. Berg to check," said Brains.

"Yeah!" said Willie. "Then called the cops to . . ."

Willie faltered to a halt.

The look McGurk was giving him—and Brains—was withering.

"If you don't *mind*," he said, "I and Joey are conducting an interrogation! . . . Mrs. Berg, could you please tell us next—"

But while McGurk may be able to glare his officers into line, there was nothing he could do about the victim herself. Not this victim, anyway.

Smiling rather sadly, she was saying:

"I'm so glad you stopped by. I've always admired you since you solved the mystery of the dead doves and saved poor Ray's cat from being blamed."

McGurk smiled back—rather sickly. He's always ready to take a little time out to be admired—even in the middle of an interrogation. What he didn't tell the lady, of course, was that she'd been one of his prime suspects in that very case!

"Gee, ma'am!" he purred. "It's nice of you to say so."

"Well I *have!*" she said. "Admired you very much —all of you. I was only thinking so this morning, before the policeman came around."

"Ma'am?"

"Yes. One of the first things I saw last night, even before I knew there'd been a break-in, was your ad thing. It had been pushed under the door. I guess I could have used your services. I probably would have, too—except I haven't been home for the past three days and didn't know about your offer."

I thought for a second there that McGurk was going to throw his arms around her neck and hug her. I mean, we may not have had any positive response to our leaflets—but here was someone admitting how useful we *might* have been. A *near-customer!*

Mrs. Berg probably didn't know it, but she had just made sure of getting our complete, wholehearted cooperation in solving the crime that had been committed against her. Absolutely free of charge, too—even if it took us months!

"Maybe we can quote what you just said on our next batch of leaflets, ma'am," McGurk said thoughtfully. "Like—'*If only I'd have hired the McGurk Organization to watch my house, a lot of my most valuable property would not have been stolen.*' But first things first. Exactly what *did* they they take, Mrs. Berg?"

⑥ Clues

"Oh, that's easy!" said Mrs. Berg. "That's what the patrolman was here for just now. To see if I'd found out exactly what is missing."

"Yes, ma'am? And have you?"

"Yes." Mrs. Berg sighed. "Just four items. But four very valuable items. Very valuable to *me*, anyway." She sighed again. "I'll say this for the thieves: They sure knew what to go for!"

"Such as what, ma'am?"

McGurk's face was a picture. A picture called *Politeness Struggling with Impatience.*

"A lovely gold watch—the pocket kind," said Mrs. Berg, her eyes beginning to fill with tears. "My husband's. They gave it to him when he retired."

"You getting this down, Joey?" McGurk asked gruffly.

I nodded.

"What else, ma'am?" he murmured.

Mrs. Berg gave a loud sniff and that seemed to bring the tears under control.

"Also—my new color TV. And my tape recorder." She reddened a little. "I've been learning to play the harmonica. I—it sounds silly, I guess, at my age. But it's something I always wanted to do and never got around to. The tape recorder was also new. I'd bought it to play back my practice tune." She managed a little laugh. "I guess the robbers won't think much of *that* when they hear it. But of course the recorder itself was worth quite a bit."

She fell silent then, looking very sad again. McGurk coughed gently.

"That's just three items, ma'am. You said there were four."

"Oh—yes! I forgot. Yes. They also took a little stash of money I had. My slush fund, I call it. Emergency money. Just one hundred and twenty dollars. In twenty-dollar bills."

"Where did you keep it?" said Brains, suddenly too interested to keep quiet, in spite of McGurk's warning scowl.

Again Mrs. Berg gave her nervous little laugh.

"In a cookie jar. In back of a shelf in the kitchen. I thought I'd been very clever, but I guess they were pretty smart."

Brains sighed noisily. He gave one of those clucks that sometimes make him sound like a teacher.

"That's just where my mother hides *her* spare cash. I'm always telling her about it. I even offered to make a special wall safe that looks like a cuckoo clock. With an electronic alarm to trigger the cuckoo. But no!"

McGurk smiled up at Mrs. Berg, part apologetic, part proud.

"Our science expert, Mrs. Berg. Officer Bellingham. The one mentioned in the leaflet. . . . Hey, come on, Joey! I thought you were taking this down."

"I am," I said. "Except I'd just like a few *hard* details, if you don't mind."

Then I turned to Mrs. Berg and got her to supply these details. Here are the notes I ended with:

CRIME : Break-in at Mrs. Berg's
PROPERTY STOLEN :
#1 Gold watch (pocket type), man's, with inscription on back :
"To Walter J. Berg, from all his many friends at Tuchman's"
#2 Color TV, 24", RCA
#3 Tape recorder, "Realistic" brand, Deluxe Battery/AC model. PLUS part-used cassette with recording of "Turkey in the Straw" (harmonica).
#4 120 dollars in cash (used 20-dollar bills, numbers unknown).

That is what *I* call a properly detailed set of notes. Even McGurk had to agree later—adding that he bet Patrolman Morelli's weren't anything near as complete.

But right then he was too busy pushing on with his interrogation.

"How did they get in, Mrs. Berg?"

"I'll show you."

She led us around the side of the house, toward the back, and pointed to a window.

"TV room," she said.

"Hmm! Well screened by this laurel bush," said Wanda.

"Did they do *that?*" said Willie, pointing to a large sheet of cardboard that had been tacked to the frame, over the bottom half of the window.

"No," said Mrs. Berg. "*I* did." For the first time, she was looking a bit angry. "The patrolman said I shouldn't have touched it before their fingerprint men had dealt with it. But I said, 'No, sir. I have a two-year-old granddaughter coming to stay with me this weekend and I don't want her cutting her fingers.' So I put cardboard on both sides." She sniffed. "And I didn't touch anything either. The broken glass is still in there, between the sheets of cardboard, stuck to the masking tape the thieves used. I didn't handle it. *I* know about fingerprints."

She was frowning at McGurk as if *he'd* raised the objection.

"Yes, ma'am. Uh—mind if we take a peek?"

He plucked at the corner of the cardboard.

"I don't see why not," said Mrs. Berg. "The patrolman did. See—the tacks are still loose at that corner."

So, very carefully, McGurk pried back the cardboard and we were able to get a good look at the burglars' workmanship.

"Neat!" murmured Brains.

"Yeah!" grunted McGurk. "Get the idea, men? They stuck this heavy-duty green masking tape all across the glass, so it wouldn't make much of a noise when they broke it—right there, under the lock."

He straightened up.

"How about inside, Mrs. Berg? Did they have to force the storm window? Or the screen?"

She shook her head.

"No. I had the storm slid up already, what with the mild weather lately. And I haven't gotten around to fixing the screens yet."

"*Toilets!*"

We all turned around, startled.

The exclamation had come from Willie. He was still bending to the broken window, with his nose poked into the gap between the cardboard and the masking tape.

"You want to use the toilet?" said Mrs. Berg. "Sure! It's—"

"No—uh—*no*, ma'am!" Willie was blushing as he straightened up. "It's just the smell I get. From in there."

"Toilets?" said Mrs. Berg, beginning to look annoyed. "Let me tell you, there's nothing wrong with *my* drains! I'm very fussy about things like that."

Willie squirmed, looking miserable.

"No, ma'am! Not the *room*. This tape stuff. And not a bad toilet smell. A *clean* one. A—a *very* clean one." He turned to me. "You know, Joey. A chemical-ly smell. Like—like—"

"Like in a *portable* toilet?" I suggested.

"Yeah! Like at summer camp!"

McGurk beamed.

"There you are, ma'am. Another specialist service. Officer Sandowsky's nose. I bet Patrolman Morelli didn't spot *that*, either."

"Yes, but what does it tell us?" said Mrs. Berg.

McGurk shrugged.

"Maybe one of the guys who broke in *deals* in portable toilets for his regular job. Or repairs them. Who knows? But it's a clue, and clues have a habit of turning out to be useful *later*."

"Correct!" said Brains. "Usually when another clue comes along, and the two of them click into place."

"Like a jigsaw puzzle," I said.

McGurk growled.

"What is this? Mrs. Berg doesn't want a course in

detective work! She wants us to catch the crooks...."

He turned to Mrs. Berg. "Did they do much damage around the house, ma'am?"

Mrs. Berg shook her head.

"No. That's the wonder of it. It was just the opposite. Everything as neat and tidy as I'd left it. Except for the broken window, of course."

"It *is* unusual," murmured Wanda.

"Whoever did it was very selective," said Mrs. Berg. "Probably gave themselves just five or ten minutes to pick up the most obviously valuable things they could see."

"Or could guess at!" said Brains, disgustedly. "Like money in a cookie jar."

"I thought at first there might be a real mess in some of the rooms," said Mrs. Berg. "As soon as I saw the TV was missing and the broken window, I thought, 'Oh dear! Vandals!' "

"But you said there was no mess, except the broken window," said McGurk.

"Yes, I know. But I was thinking about the mess I'd *already* found. Out in the driveway, when I got back. Garbage all over the place. It took me a half-hour to clean it all up this morning."

"Oh, *that*!" said Brains. "No, Mrs. Berg. That was done by some little kids. They've been doing it all over the neighborhood for these past few days."

"So I heard," said Mrs. Berg. "Well, anyway, no little kids carried that TV out, I'll tell you! And no little kids knew how to make such a careful selection."

"No-o-o!" said McGurk, very slowly. "But. . . ."

He didn't finish his thought. There was a strange gleam in his eyes all at once.

And suddenly he was anxious for us to leave. No kidding! I mean, it was the very first time I'd known him to be impatient to leave the scene of a crime!

What he said next really made me wonder.

"Come on, men! You saw Officer Morelli and the way he brushed us off just now. Well, he's right. This is a job for the police, not kids. *We* should be concentrating on the *kids'* crime—the garbage vandals."

Mrs. Berg sighed and said, "Yes, I suppose you're right."

But she didn't know McGurk the way we did.

Willie gaped. Brains's glasses began to slide down his nose. Wanda gasped. I nearly dropped my notebook.

McGurk ignored all these signs of astonishment.

McGurk was already on his way!

7 More Break-Ins

"Hey, McGurk!" said Wanda, as we hurried to catch up with him out on the street. "Are you feeling all right?"

She sounded concerned rather than sarcastic.

McGurk didn't slow down.

"We've no time to waste, men," he said. "I've got a hunch."

"Really?" said Wanda, still not sarcastic.

(McGurk's hunches are to be taken seriously at all times.)

"What hunch?" Willie asked respectfully.

"Can't go into it now," said McGurk. "What we have to do *now*—" His pace was still fast, but erratic—not quite so fast as he passed each driveway and glanced at it. "What we have to do now is make a lightning tour of the neighborhood. Look out for places that still have garbage in the driveway—"

He glanced at another. It was clean. He picked up speed again.

"And when we come to them—you, Joey—you make a note of them. A careful note. Each place. Which we then investigate further."

So far, all the driveways had been clean. Some of them, we knew for a fact, had had the cans spilled there the day before. But the mess had been cleared up within hours, maybe even minutes.

"Why?" said Willie. "What are we doing *this* for? We could be checking up on the chemical smell clue."

"I think *I* see why," said Brains. "The chemical smell clue's no good unless we get something else— some more jigsaw pieces that come in between. What McGurk's trying to do is—"

"Here's one!" said McGurk, cutting out all further chat.

He led us up a driveway, sidestepping empty cans and bottles and bulging plastic garbage bags. The house looked deserted, but McGurk went straight up to the front door and pressed the bell.

He pressed it two more times and knocked on the door for good measure.

When there was still no reply, he said:

"Right, men. You getting the address down, Joey? . . . Good. Now we look around. We check. Thoroughly. Using our special skills. Just as if the owners had hired us."

Well, we found nothing wrong at *that* house. All first-floor windows and doors were secure. No lurkers or loiterers. No suspicious smells.

"O.K.," said McGurk, looking only a little disappointed. "It hasn't been broken into." He glanced at my notes. The page was headed: PLACES WITH GARBAGE MESS IN DRIVEWAY. Then came the address of this one. "Make that List *A*, Joey. But save a clean page for List *B*."

"List *B*?" I said, not too pleased at having him tell me *my* job.

"Yeah!" he said grimly. "Places with garbage mess in the driveway that also show signs of having been broken into!"

He certainly has faith in his hunches, I'll say that!

And at our very next check, he was proved right. It didn't take any special skill to see it, either.

A small frosted window at the back had been

broken. The shattered pieces were still sticking to the strips of masking tape that hung there.

Green masking tape.

"Looks like—gosh!"

Brains had turned pale all of a sudden.

"Never mind what it *looks* like," said McGurk. "What does it *smell* like, Willie?"

Very cautiously, as if he expected a hairy hand to shoot out from the hole and grab his nose, Willie sniffed.

"Same," he said. "Yeah. Exactly. Same chemical smell."

"What do we do now?" said Wanda. "Call the police?"

"Not yet," said McGurk. "It's too late to prevent the robbery *now*. These guys—the real thieves—work after dark, if my hunch is correct. . . . No. Just make a careful note of it, Joey, and we'll see if there are any more. That's the first thing. When we hand the cops the list I want it to be *complete*. O.K.?"

We agreed.

The house was very silent, but none of us was eager to follow in the burglars' footsteps and go through that window to check inside.

And McGurk's plan seemed to pay off at first.

There *were* more.

Two more.

Like the first one (and also Mrs. Berg's), they both had broken windows at the back of the house, with strips of green masking tape—and the tape had the same chemical smell. (According to Willie. I mean *I* couldn't smell anything and I don't think any of the others did. But Willie's nose—well, you just have to go along with it if *he* says it has picked up some scent. I've learned that much by now.)

Anyway, here are my notes for these break-ins:

HOUSES WITH GARBAGE MESSES —

(B) WITH SIGNS OF FORCED ENTRY.

(Not counting Mrs. Berg's.)

#1   293 East Melon

#2   37 East Sheridan

#3   95 East Olive   ? machine-Gun Kelly's?

That last house had a very special interest for us, as you might guess from the rather startled query I scribbled after it. (Not like my *usual* neat style, please note!)

It was a very big old Spanishy type house, similar to Mrs. Kranz's. Only a block away, in fact—though that wasn't why it had this special interest. No. As I say, it was big and old, with a large overgrown yard where an army could have lurked and loitered. This wild state was understandable, since the house had been standing empty for almost a year.

Now, however, the windows were clean, with new drapes—and when we peeked inside we could see there was new furniture there.

"You know who's taken this place, don't you?" said Wanda, suddenly sounding worried, as we stood looking at the broken window at the back.

We others shook our heads.

"No. Who?"

"Mr. Kelly," she said.

"Not—?" Willie's jaw dropped.

"Yes," said Wanda. "The new Junior High principal. He and his wife moved in last week. I guess they're taking a short vacation before he starts his new job."

We all fell silent for a bit—and that's when I scrawled my anxious query. I mean, Mr. Kelly—Mr. Justin Kelly—Mr. *Machine-Gun* Kelly as we'd started to call him—he was a guy to be reckoned with.

We'd clashed with him only a few months ago, when he'd come with his wife to look around the town just before New Year's. This was while we were investigating bank robberies, and McGurk had mistaken him for the driver of a getaway car, waiting outside a bank. McGurk being McGurk, he'd ordered us to do something about it—something pretty drastic, which I have described already in *The Case of the Bashful Bank Robber*. It might have worked out fine—if Mr. Kelly really had been the driver of a getaway car. But it was Mrs. Kelly, not some gun-toting crooks, who had come out of the bank. And she had caught us in the act.

The Kellys hadn't admired our public spirit one

little bit. They thought we'd just been fooling around and Mr. Kelly told us he'd remember our faces. He said even if another year did go by before we went to his school, he'd still remember us. Mr. "Elephant" Kelly might have been another good name for him, but someone mentioned the old bank robber, Machine-Gun Kelly, and I guess that stuck.

Anyway, just the *thought* of him had made most of us look worried.

Except McGurk.

His face shone.

"You don't say! You *sure*?"

Wanda nodded.

"Positive. My cousin Amy works at the furniture store where they bought the new drapes and rugs."

McGurk rubbed his hands together.

"Well this is our big chance to get in good with him. Catch the thieves who've broken in. There's no telling what valuable new items they'll have swiped."

"Yes, but how?" said Wanda. "We can't go *in* there, looking for clues. That's a police job. You said so yourself to Mrs. Berg."

"Sure!" said McGurk. "But we don't *need* to go inside. The best clues are out here." He pointed to the garbage—dry stuff mainly: old paint cans and strips of wallpaper, some of which had been blown into the bushes. "*These* will lead us to the burglars!"

"How?" Wanda repeated.

Before anyone else could jump in with the answer, McGurk said:

"This was the hunch I was telling you about! And it's paying off in a big way."

Then he went into his explanation, and I must admit it was terrific. As we stood there, at the side of the smashed window, among the garbage and the straggling bushes, all our attention was focused on Jack P. McGurk.

Which was very nearly our undoing.

8 The Four Flying Fingers— and Thumb

I have to admit that his explanation showed Mc-Gurk's detective brain working in top form.

"Those four kids," he said. "Knocking over the garbage cans. They weren't *vandalizing*. They were *fingering!*"

That shook us all, I can tell you. Even Brains, who seemed to have had some idea of what McGurk was driving at earlier.

"Fingering?" he said.

"Yes," said McGurk, his eyes shining. "They've been pointing out the houses where the people are away. So that those houses can be burglarized at leisure."

"But—but, *McGurk!*" said Wanda. "They were too

young! You heard what Mrs. Berg said. They couldn't have handled that big TV set."

"And they'd probably have made a bigger mess *inside* the house," said Brains.

McGurk wasn't shaken one little bit by these objections. In fact he even *relished* them. You could tell by the way his grin broadened with each one.

"Not the garbage kids!" he said, when we were through. "*They* didn't do the breaking in. They were fingering for someone else. Someone older. Someone who *would* be suspected if he went around snooping in the ordinary way."

Then all at once I could see it. It was beautiful. It even gave me the idea for what to call the case.

"The Case of the Four Flying Fingers!" I said.

"Eh?"

McGurk stared at me, puzzled.

"Not the Galloping Garbage Gang you thought was so funny, McGurk. No. *The Four Flying Fingers!*"

His face lit up again.

"Hey! Yeah! Good thinking, Officer Rockaway!"

Then of course he had to top it. Looking stern again, he said:

"And, by Sherlock, it's our job to track down The Thumb!"

Willie started back from the broken window.

"*What* thumb?" he said, peering down, as if he expected to see blood stains. "You think he cut his thumb off, McGurk?"

"No, Willie. The Thumb's the guy who comes around later to see where the junk is still on the driveway. All he has to do then is go boldly up to the front door and use his thumb."

"How?" said Willie.

"On the doorbell. Just to make sure. If anyone *does* answer, all he needs do is ask if they realize there's all this garbage on their driveway. Like he's a Good Samaritan type."

"Isn't that stretching it a bit too far, McGurk?" said Wanda.

"Yes," said Brains. "Wouldn't that risk drawing attention to his own link with the garbage? Later? After the break-in? When the people began to think about it?"

McGurk started to look mad.

"What does it matter *what* excuse he makes? He knows better than to burglarize the places where people *do* answer the door. But if the garbage has been left on the driveway, the chances are no one will answer anyway. And *that's* the main thing."

"Sure!" I said, soothingly. "Go on, McGurk."

"Then The Thumb knows for *sure* there's nobody home. *Plus.* . . ." (Here a look of indescribable cunning crossed McGurk's face. It's the look that always reminds me that inside every great detective brain, there's another brain—imprisoned but put to good use. The brain of a master criminal.) *"Plus,"* he said, "it tells him the neighbors aren't especially interested or alert. Otherwise *they'd* have cleared up the mess."

This made Wanda look troubled.

"Maybe *we* should do it," she said. "At those houses where there's garbage but which still haven't been broken into."

"Yes," I said, reaching for my notebook. "I have the addresses—"

"Later, later!" said McGurk, waving my book aside. "There's no urgency yet. Not until it's dark. And long before then we're gonna crack this case, men. Right now, we—"

But whatever else he had in mind, right *then* we did two things. First, we froze, for about five seconds. Then, led by McGurk, we made a crouching run along the side of the house and into the deepest tangle of bushes and old long grass we could find.

We froze because of the voice:

"Hey! What are you *doing* in there?"

A woman's voice. Coming from a thinner part of the hedge toward the far corner of the bottom of the back yard.

I could just see the blur of her face through the twigs, and the flash of her glasses.

"What's wrong, Bertha?"

A deeper voice—a man's. Another blur, approaching the first one.

"Some kids, Clyde. Over in the new teacher's yard. I think they're up to no good."

That was enough for McGurk.

"Quick!" he said. "Out of sight! Now!"

So that's when we followed him—moving even faster when we heard the tromp of footsteps crashing through twigs and undergrowth behind us.

McGurk's instincts were right, I suppose. I mean, suspicious as it looked, our running like that, it would have looked even worse to be caught there in the open, at the side of the busted window. Caught and carefully *identified*—putting the wrong ideas into those people's heads.

McGurk was right too in diving into the nearest cover. Because by the time we'd done that, the man had come pounding around the side of the house, scattering the empty cans as he ran to the end of the driveway. If we'd taken *that* route, he'd have been sure to get a good look at some of us, running away on the open street.

For a second or two there, with Willie's breath tickling the back of my neck and some kind of bug crawling over my hand, I thought the guy himself might be putting two and two together. Like when he didn't see us out there, it might cross his mind to search the yard.

But luckily his wife called out just then.

"Clyde! Come quickly! *Clyde!*"

Her voice was rising to a scream.

"Coming, honey!" he said.

And we breathed easier.

But not for long.

"*Look!*" we heard her say. "This window! They were breaking in!"

"You sure? You saw them doing it?"

"No. But they were standing right here. Talking in low voices. That's what made me suspicious."

"You get a good look at them?"

"Well . . . not very good. What with all the twigs. But there were four or five of them."

"Kids?"

"Yes."

"The same bunch who knocked our garbage can over?"

"Well, maybe. Except one was a girl this time, I'm sure of it." Next to me, Wanda gave a kind of choking gasp. "And I think one of the boys had a red-and-black shirt—sort of stripey." Willie's nose nearly blew my right ear off, it gave out such a blast of air. I heard him fumbling around, fastening his windbreaker right up to his chin. "And—well—that's about all I could see."

A ripple of relief went through the rest of us.

"Anyway, it looks like you spotted 'em in time, Bertha. So now we'll go right back and call the police."

As soon as their footsteps faded, we did the same. Faded through the undergrowth and out into the street, where—urged by McGurk—we strolled, as casually as we could, but very, very stiffly and jerkily, back to Headquarters.

"We have to think about this carefully, men," he murmured, once we'd reached his yard. "Otherwise things could look very black for us."

"Very black indeed!" I grunted, seeing exactly where his thoughts were headed.

9 McGurk's Gamble

"So this was going to be our big chance to get in good with Mr. Kelly!" said Wanda, once we were safely behind the closed door of our HQ. "*Fat chance!*"

"Yes," said Brains. "It's going to look pretty bad for us if that woman identifies us."

"Do you think she will?" asked Willie, with the windbreaker still fastened up to his neck.

"No way!" jeered McGurk. "You heard what she said. She didn't get a good enough look at us. And even if she had—well, you know how hard it is to make an accurate ID. Even for *trained* observers, like us."

We had to go along with that.

"Still and all," said Wanda, with a sigh, "I think we ought to get in first with *our* story. Tell the police everything we know."

I agreed.

"It makes sense, McGurk. Especially the information about the other two break-ins. The ones that no one else knows about yet."

"*Not* to tell the police about them is an offense," said Brains. "Isn't it?"

"Yes," I said. "Withholding information about a criminal act."

"So let's phone the police right now," said Wanda, standing up.

"*Wait!*" said McGurk.

His face had turned red. His eyes were angry. His mouth was scornful.

"*Jerks!*" he said. "What d'you think that would do to our image? As a security service? Huh?"

"But—"

"If we tell the cops *now*, we'll be ordered off the case. Sure—we might get some praise for *finding out* about the break-ins. But what sort of security service does that make *us*? More like a *bad news* service!"

"I can see that, McGurk," said Brains. "But what else *can* we do?"

McGurk looked grim now—grim and determined. His eyes were focused on some point above our heads.

"We can do what I was saying back in the Kellys' yard. We can go ahead and collar the perpetrators ourselves. If we act quickly we can have it all wrapped up by the end of the day."

"You mean by tracking down the kids?" I said.

"Right!" said McGurk. His eyes came back to study our faces. "Those kids. They're the key. . . . Recognize any of them? Any of you?"

We were shaking our heads and frowning.

"They don't live around *here*," said Wanda. "Not in this immediate area, anyway."

"Anyone recognize them from *school* then?" McGurk asked. "You, Brains. They were closer to your age. Remember seeing them *there*?"

Brains flushed a little. He's kind of touchy about his age. Just turned ten, he's a whole year younger than the rest of us.

"I don't pay much attention to the little kids," he said. "In fact I don't think anyone does. At school you get to know the names and faces of kids in higher grades, but the younger ones—" He shrugged. "That's how *my* mind works, anyway."

"Mine too!" said Wanda.

"Yeah!" muttered Willie.

McGurk glared at me.

"You, too, Joey?"

I nodded. I didn't like to admit it, but Brains had a point there.

"So how about *you*, McGurk?" said Wanda. "I suppose you've memorized the names and faces and addresses of *every* kid at school—older *and* younger?"

He brushed that one aside.

"No," he said. "But I do know when I *haven't* seen a face before. So my guess is that those kids come from another part of town and that they go to school *there*. And my bet, men"—he looked around wisely—"is that they're from the North side."

Brains caught his breath.

"You mean where—?"

"Where there's already been a rash of break-ins," said McGurk. "Yeah!"

It was beginning to look as if he was right again!

He hunched forward.

"So here's what we do, men. Right after this, we patrol the whole town—north, south, east, west. Every neighborhood."

"But that's a big area!"

"Sure! That's why we do it on bikes. And anyway,

it isn't as big as it sounds. I mean, unless those kids are taking the day off, we probably won't find them on the North side. That's already been covered by The Thumb. Same with this neighborhood. So we concentrate on the other neighborhoods—where they haven't been active yet."

"On bikes?" said Willie.

"Sure!" said McGurk. "The Four Flying Fingers are going to meet the McGurk Organization Flying *Squad*. We fight speed with speed, men!"

Well by now he'd gotten us all raring to go again. It was a big gamble he was proposing. I mean, if we *didn't* catch up with those kids by the end of the day, the outlook for us could be even blacker than it was already, what with withholding information and all. But the idea of a Flying Squad was too good to pass up.

"O.K., McGurk," I said. "I'm ready to give it a try."

"Me too!" said Willie.

"And I," murmured Brains.

"Officer Grieg?" said McGurk.

"On one condition," said Wanda. "I still don't like the idea of being arrested for withholding evidence."

"So?"

"So we phone the police and tell them about the broken windows on East Melon and East Sheridan."

McGurk looked ready to explode. I thought he might suspend Wanda from duty and demand the return of her ID card.

"Now you listen to *me*, Officer—"

"Hold it, McGurk!" said Wanda. "I'm not suggesting we give our names. I'm suggesting we tip them off anonymously. Disguising our voices. You're good at that, aren't you?"

If ever a facial expression can be said to turn a

complete somersault, McGurk's did then. In those few seconds, Officer Grieg's position changed likewise. From being handed a Dishonorable Discharge to being promoted to Assistant Chief—it happened in one leap.

"Wanda!" cried McGurk. "You're a genius! . . . Come on, men. We'll do it right now, while my folks are still out shopping."

The McGurks' phone is one of those with extraloud receivers. McGurk's grandmother often comes to stay with them and she's rather deaf and the phone was fixed that way for her benefit. It was McGurk himself who suggested it, in fact. Thoughtful of him? Not really. You see, in McGurk's eyes (or ears) that is the next best thing to those open telephone receivers you see on TV, when the police chiefs just press a button and don't even bother to hold the phones to their heads.

That's why I am able to give you an exact transcript of the call McGurk made to police headquarters that morning. What I am *not* able to show very well in the transcript is the weird, croaky, muffled voice that McGurk used, wrapping one of his mother's silk scarves over the mouthpiece.

But here goes. Starting with when McGurk got a reply from one of the cops on duty.

(Remember, McGurk's part sounded muffled, scratchy, with a terrible accent.)

McGURK: Now I'm only gonna say this once, so listen and listen good.

COP: Hello! Could you speak a little clearer, please?

McGURK: I'm only gonna say this once so listen and listen good!

COP: I'm sorry, sir. We must have a bad line here. What was that you said?

McGURK: I'M ONLY GONNA SAY THIS ONCE SO LISTEN AND--

COP: O.K., O.K.! I hear you, son. Go on.

Well, that change from "sir" to "son" says it all. In his desperation, McGurk had started to shed his disguise. The rest of us began to shuffle around uneasily. Wanda looked as if she was wondering if her idea had been such a good one, after all.

But somehow McGurk managed to croak out his information without giving away *too* much of his identity.

Even so. . . .

Here's how the conversation ended.

```
COP:     Well, thanks, son. We'll look into
         the matter. You sure you don't want
         to give your name?

McGURK:  If I did that, they'd find out and
         kill me. They- they got my wife and
         little daughter. They'd kill them, too!

COP:     Hey, now, come on!. . . Haven't I heard
         your voice someplace before? I mean if
         this turns out to be a gag, son-
```

And there—much to our relief—McGurk hung up.

"Well, men," he said, grinning broadly, "no one can say we withheld evidence *now*."

"No," murmured Wanda. "Except that I'm not sure that that cop won't be able to put a name to the voice, once he starts thinking about it. It wasn't one of your *best* disguises, McGurk."

McGurk's grin slipped a little. Then:

"So what?" he said. "That's all the more reason for us to grab our bikes and start looking for those kids right away!"

10 The Flying Squad

There was still over an hour to go before lunch, and it didn't take us long to get our bikes and gather outside HQ. In those few minutes, McGurk had had time to think.

Now when McGurk is really onto something, he thinks fast and he thinks well. So it didn't surprise me to find he'd gotten our tactical moves all worked out.

"We've never used our bikes in this way before, men," he said, waving a sheet of typing paper. "So here's how we proceed."

Then he showed us his plan.

Well, I have to be fair about this. That plan was

a winner. On paper. It was so good that I kept a
copy for our records. Here's the first part:

```
THE MᶜGURK ORGANIZATION
      FLYING SQUAD
OPERATIONAL  PROCEDURE
Phase # 1 (Search)
         I McG
    Wa I    I Wi
    B I    I J
```

McGurk explained it like this:

"That's us on our bikes, O.K.? With me out front,
leading. Wanda and Willie come next, side by side,
about ten feet behind. Then, bringing up the rear
—you and Brains, Joey. Another ten feet. Got that?"

We nodded.

"That, of course, is only the *search* pattern. While
we are cruising around, looking for the perpetrators.
Once they are sighted, we go straight into Phase
Two. Hard and fast."

We studied Phase Two. Here it is:

"What's *appre*-whosis mean?" asked Willie.

"Apprehension," I said. "The capture."

"Right," said McGurk, "The collar. The four crosses are the perpetrators. This is how we box them in at the side of a wall or fence or hedge. If we do this quick enough and tight enough, men, they won't have time to scatter."

Well, as I say, the plan looked good. No one raised any objections. We were all too eager to whizz out onto the streets and put it into action.

But I also said: *on paper.*

It wasn't long before we realized the difference. I mean it was all right for McGurk, out front on his own. And it might have been all right if we'd all had lots of practice and were riding the same kinds of bikes.

But Wanda had borrowed her brother Ed's ten-speed model, while Willie was riding an old bone-shaker that had been rusting in his garage all winter. That was one reason they found it so hard to keep side by side at all times, exactly ten feet behind our leader. In fact Wanda's bike kept surging ahead so fast that it began to look like we had *two* leaders. Meanwhile, Willie kept wobbling to a standstill, making Brains and me fall back with him —the three of us lagging more like thirty feet behind.

Another reason for breaking the pattern laid down by McGurk was traffic.

I'm not saying the streets were crowded with cars, like in a big city. But there were enough of them around to make us slip into single file every few blocks, and then get into all kinds of tangles sorting ourselves out again.

I tell you—after half an hour McGurk was fit to be tied. He kept yelling at us to keep to the plan, and we kept yelling back at him and at each other —and, honestly, if those kids had been anywhere around, yelling and knocking over a *million* garbage cans, we would never have seen or heard them.

But by lunchtime we were beginning to get the

hang of it. So much so that, after lunch, when we'd
started patrolling a neighborhood over to the east
and McGurk spotted the Flying Fingers, the Flying Squad was in perfect formation.

We'd already sensed that we were getting warm.
Inside ten minutes, we'd spotted five houses where
the people were angrily cleaning up garbage in
their driveways—people who'd obviously been home
when they heard the crash, and had dashed right
out to deal with the mess.

So it was no surprise when McGurk raised his
right hand and, pointing ahead, called out:

"There they go, men!"

The setup was perfect. I've been thinking about it since, and the main criticism I have about Phase Two of McGurk's plan is this:

How can we be sure that every time we catch up with a bunch of perpetrators, they'll be at the side of a high wall or fence, ready to be boxed in?

I mean, McGurk's plan might be good for cars, with the side of the road acting as a natural barrier. But kids? On foot? They could have been spread out—some one side of the street, some the other. And even if they'd been together on the sidewalk, there might have been nothing much to stop them from jumping over into the yards at the edge.

But no. That afternoon, we'd gotten lucky.

For there were the four kids, close together, on the sidewalk, next to a high long fence. And they weren't even running. The houses were well spaced out in this part of town and the Flying Fingers must have been taking a breather. In fact they'd come to a halt when we spotted them. The kid with the feather in his headband was looking at some paper the kid with the hat was holding. And the other two were studying it, too.

Perfect.

I mean, there *we* were, alert, in correct formation; and there *they* were, unsuspecting, positioned just right for a collar. Everything was set for us to go into Phase Two. Hard and fast.

On paper.

Because once more the snag was *other* activities going on in the vicinity. I guess that's why they always clear the streets first when shooting such scenes with cars in TV movies.

McGurk went in beautifully. He crashed broadside across the sidewalk in front of the kids and leaped off his bike yelling through the still-spinning wheels: *"Freeze! You're under arrest!"*

We others moved in according to plan.

But the plan didn't account for another element. An old guy walking a young dog, just behind McGurk. I guess they could have been shown on the plan as a V.

That was the *shape* they made, anyway.

When McGurk came screaming and crashing to a stop, the old gentleman and his dog were only about five or six feet farther up the sidewalk. The dog—a frisky young dalmatian—must have thought this was the best thing since canned dogfood. He jumped joyously forward to join the fun, rearing up at the end of the leash. The old guy, on the other hand, must have thought World War Three had broken out, and an enemy paratrooper had

landed in front of him. *He* stepped back, alarmed. He might even have fallen over backward if it hadn't been for the dog lunging forward.

So there you have it. A model of the way even the best plans can go wrong.

Ending with the old guy regaining his balance and giving McGurk and the dog the biggest bawling-out either of them had ever had in their lives.

And the Four Flying Fingers?

They loved it!

They stood there gawking and grinning and lapping up every word the old man laid on McGurk. I mean those kids were taken by surprise, every bit as much as the man and his dog—so much so that they didn't even realize they were the original targets!

Run and scatter?

No, sir!

When the old guy was through with McGurk and had gone grumbling on his way, tugging the reluctant pup with him, the kid with the feather stepped up to McGurk and said:

"Hey, man! That was neat! What game are *you* playing? *Attack from Outer Space?*"

McGurk just glared at him.

"You're under arrest!" he snarled.

11 McGurk Makes a Deal

"Arrest? *Us?*" The leader stared at McGurk, still grinning. "You kidding?"

"No!" growled McGurk.

The leader laughed. His feather shook. He turned to the others.

"Hear that, fellas? This freak from outer space says he isn't kidding. He wants to *arrest* us!"

The hat boy tried to grin back. He had big front teeth and he licked them nervously.

"Let's move on, Sam. We—"

"Yes," muttered one of the other kids—a very dark, very slight kid with steel-frame glasses. "You talk too much, Sam."

The fourth boy just stared dopily, first at his

leader, then at ours, as if he didn't know what was going on.

"No," said the feather kid, the one they called Sam. "Let's hear this freak out. Arrest us for *what*?"

"The garbage cans—" McGurk began.

"The garbage cans! Now that *is* garbage!"

"Are you trying to tell us you haven't been knocking them over?"

"No," said the leader. "But it's just a game, that's all." He sneered. "*Arrest* us!"

"I suppose you're going to say you were only playing Cowboys and Indians?" said Wanda.

"Well—" the dopey one began.

"Or Cops and Robbers?" said McGurk. "Well now *you're* copped."

Sam was still sneering.

"You want to know what's dumb, Jackie? This is dumb. Watch their faces when I tell them what we *really* were playing."

"Sam, I don't think—"

But Sam wasn't about to listen to any advice from his henchmen—and that's where I began to notice certain similarities between him and you-know-who.

"The game we were playing, *copper*," he said, "is called Nickel-a-Can."

That threw McGurk a little. He blinked.

"You mean Kick-the-Can?"

"No. *Nickel*-a-Can. We get a nickel for every can we knock over. Jackie here keeps the score. Show 'em, Jackie."

Jackie tilted back his hat and sighed. Then he pulled out of his pocket the paper we'd seen them all looking at when we'd first spotted them. Only it wasn't just paper. It was a notebook—grubbier, more crumpled, *but otherwise just like mine!*

"Here!" muttered Jackie, giving Sam a despairing look.

We stared at the page it was folded over at. I am able to show the exact piece of evidence, and here it is:

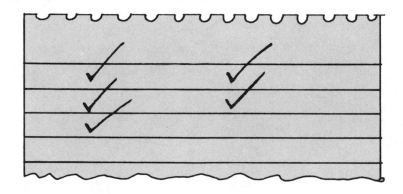

"Every tick gets us a nickel," said Sam.

The dopey one giggled.

"A nickel a tickle!" he said.

The other Fingers looked at him in surprise. He obviously didn't come up with such smart cracks every day.

Then Sam turned back to McGurk.

"See? Nickel-a-Can." He bent forward confidentially, so that his feather brushed McGurk's freckles. "And listen," he said. "You look like a smart guy. I like your style. So what we'll do, we'll cut you in. One cent in every nickel goes to you."

McGurk backed away. A mixture of outrage and amazement was struggling on his face. For once he was speechless!

Sam must have misread it. Maybe he thought McGurk was overcome by the generosity of his offer.

"But you gotta *earn* it," he said. "Like if anyone chases us and looks like he's catching up—you ride your bikes in the way."

"Yeah," said the little one with glasses, suddenly fired. "Or pick us up. Like the bikes were getaway cars."

Oh boy! I thought. This was getting a bit spooky. I mean, the Flying Fingers were turning out to be some kind of shadowy, crooked version of the Mc-Gurk Organization! With Sam reminding me of McGurk, Jackie and his notebook reminding me of me, the dumb one reminding me a bit of Willie— and now *this*.

Because the way the dark kid with the glasses had just blinked up at his leader was *exactly* like the look Brains sometimes gives McGurk.

I was beginning to wonder if they had a sister hanging around someplace—a shadow Wanda!

But McGurk had gotten his speech back.

"*That*," he said, "is bribery and corruption. That's *another* charge—"

"Come off it! You're not real cops!"

"Maybe," said McGurk. "But we can make a citizen's arrest. And that's just what we're doing. Right now."

"What for? A *game*?"

"Littering the public highway, for one thing."

"Just a sec!" The kid with the glasses was getting to act and look like Brains more than ever. Cool. Wise. Solemn. "Those weren't public highways. They were private driveways."

"Interference with private property then!" Mc-Gurk snarled. "Pollution! Littering when some of it *does* blow into the street. And of course—" he slowed down, giving every word its full weight— *"felonious breaking and entering."*

That made Sam's jaw sag. The feather tilted back.

"Fellow-what? We—we never broke and entered nothing! Except garbage cans!"

He was beginning to sound like a frightened little boy now.

Wanda stepped forward. She must have seen her chance.

"Let me take over, McGurk," she said softly. "Like with Bèla that time," she added, even more softly.

I saw what she was getting at. She'd used the same technique on another frightened little kid, in the Phantom Frog case, and it had paid off.

McGurk must have seen this, too.

"Go on, then!" he said, gruffly.

Wanda bent down a little, to bring her eyes level with Sam's.

"Look," she said. "We don't want to get you into trouble. But this game, this Nickel-a-Can. Who gives you the nickels?"

Sam frowned, then shrugged.

"The lady."

"Which lady?"

Sam glanced at his buddies, then dropped his head and shrugged again.

"Lady in a camper," he muttered.

"*Chemical toilets!*" cried Brains.

Everyone stared at him, including his own "shadow."

"Huh?" said Willie.

"The *smell!*" said Brains. "It fits. *Campers* have chemical toilets. He's telling the truth!"

"O.K., O.K.!" muttered McGurk. "Wanda? You want to go ahead?"

Wanda nodded.

"What camper?" she asked. "Where?"

Sam shrugged again.

"Don't know. She just drives around. Meets us on the street. Some kinda nut. She says it's a service she's making—"

"A *survey!*" said the kid with the hat.

"Yeah, that's what I said. A survey. To see how fast folks are at cleaning up their driveways. How *really* neat people are."

"But she's *honest*," said the kid with glasses. "She always pays us. Never argues."

"What does she look like?" said Wanda.

Sam frowned.

"Just—just a lady. Long hair. Kinda like yours."

Oh boy! I thought, getting that spooky feeling again.

I decided to bring this back to the level of hard facts.

"Did you get the number of the camper?"

Still another shrug.

"Why should I? . . . Did any of you guys?"

The other three Fingers shook their heads.

"Will you be seeing her again today?" said Mc-Gurk.

"No. We already did. She paid us for yesterday and told us where she'd like to see the spilled garbage today." Sam's grin began to return, hesitantly. "You *sure* you don't want a piece of the action?"

"*No!*" said McGurk. "And the *action* can stop right now. You go right back to where you came from and you don't do any of this anymore. Or you're in big trouble."

Jackie sniffed.

"You don't even know *where* we come from!"

I wasn't about to take this. Not from my shadow!

"No," I said. "But we can soon find out!"

I snatched the notebook from his hand. McGurk and Willie stepped forward to block his attempt to grab the book back.

"*Can't* we, *Jackie Widlow?*" I said, reading from

the name and address he'd written on the front cover—just where I write mine (only more neatly). "Here's his address, McGurk," I said. "Name, street, number, city, state, zip code—even *The Earth*, and *The World*, and *The Universe*," I added, reading aloud. Then I couldn't help flipping through the pages and—sure enough—the little creep seemed to have something like my own orderly mind!

Here's a specimen:

```
Friday Take
32 cans = $1.60
  Share out -
  Sam H.    40¢
  Lonny J.  40¢
  Merv J.   40¢
  Jackie N. 40¢
```

I showed that one to McGurk. He smiled and took the book from me.

"We'll keep this as evidence," he said. "You've

got yourself a good bookkeeper, Sam K., Lonny T., Merv J." Then he glared at them and tapped the book. "Any more cans get knocked over and this goes to the cops. We can soon trace you through this. Now beat it."

He must have decided what I'd decided already. The kids had to be telling the truth. They knew nothing about the break-ins, otherwise they'd never have blabbed about the Nickel-a-Can deal in the first place. Also—if they'd known they were mixed up in something as serious as burglary—they would certainly have given McGurk a harder time over that book. They were too young to know that McGurk was bluffing. Even Jackie Widlow wasn't smart enough to remind our leader that you couldn't seize evidence like that without a warrant. But they *would* have raised a bigger yell.

No. These were just mischievous little kids and Sam had been telling the truth. To them it really *was* just a game. A nuisance game, sure—but nothing worse. With the McGurk Organization, nothing more than a bunch of older kids—spoilsports—playing another kind of game.

They began to drift off, grumbling among themselves.

"Hey!" McGurk called out. They stopped. "If

you do see the camper lady today, no word about this. O.K.?"

Sam must have seen a glimmer of hope. His grin came back. He adjusted his feather so it stuck up high.

"Or what?"

"Or this notebook goes to the cops just the same."

Sam glared back at McGurk. He glanced at his buddies. Here was a guy desperate not to lose any more face.

"And if we see her and *don't* tell her?"

McGurk must have sensed Sam's problem too. He grinned.

"This notebook—this evidence—gets destroyed."

Sam's grin was even broader than McGurk's. I could see he was suddenly beginning to enjoy this new game, after all.

"O.K., copper," he said, raising his hand in an Indian-type salute. "You got yourself a deal!"

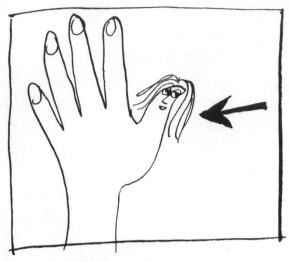

12 Lady Thumb

McGurk's next decision was very smart. He made it when Wanda asked what we should do next.

"We stay over here," he said. "On the East side. Right here, where she told the Fingers to operate today. She's sure to be cruising around before long, looking out for where the garbage hasn't been cleaned up."

"She's going to be disappointed," said Brains. "I don't think the kids had done much before we caught up with them."

"Yes," I said. "Maybe it'll make her suspicious."

McGurk shook his head thoughtfully. Then he showed once more how good he was at second-guessing the criminal mind.

"Not necessarily," he said. "She'll just think more folks are home today, ready to clean up the mess. Or maybe that the Fingers are having an off-day. The last thing she'll think of is that they've been collared and spilled everything they know."

"Why's that, McGurk?" asked Willie.

"Because she is one overconfident lady. She's had this terrific idea and she thinks it's fireproof. Maybe it would have been, at that—if it hadn't been for me spotting it."

There spoke one overconfident *boy*, I thought.

But basically McGurk's plan made sense, and none of us protested when he had us patrolling that area, making it look casual, like we were out for a Saturday afternoon bike ride and weren't sure exactly which way to go.

And it paid off. In just over a half-hour we saw the cream-colored camper—also patrolling the area, also making it look casual, like the driver wasn't sure where some friend lived.

"That's *got* to be it!" said McGurk, stopping as the camper came slowly along the street. "Quick, men. Pretend to be looking at my front tire. Like it might be springing a slow leak."

I guess the driver must have been too busy looking out for garbage to give us more than a glance.

I mean, if she had she'd have been sure to get suspicious—overconfident or not.

Yes, we were crouching over McGurk's front wheel all right. But out from between the spokes, over the handlebars and across the saddle, five pairs of eyes were staring directly at *her*—not at any slow leak.

Sam had been right. Her hair did look sort of like Wanda's. Long, and dusty blond. But there the likeness ended. Wanda's is a kind of pleasant face, even when she's mad. This woman's face was good-looking enough, I guess, but you'd never call it pleasant. It was long and thin, with high sharp cheekbones and a pointed chin. It was deeply tanned and it reminded me of a wolf's face. The arm that rested on the sill of the window as she drove slowly along was also deeply tanned and lean—and it had blue tattoo marks. I don't know about overconfident, but this was certainly one very *tough* lady.

"Lady Thumb!" McGurk whispered. "It *has* to be."

Now maybe he said, "*That's* the lady Thumb!" But his whisper was so low, it sounded to me like "Lady Thumb." The others must have thought so too, because that's how we all referred to her from that moment on.

"O.K., men," said McGurk, when she'd turned the next corner. "She isn't going so fast. So we follow her *Except—*" Wanda had just started to surge ahead. She checked. *"Except we keep our distance!"* McGurk commanded. "That's a lady you can't fool for very long."

We nodded. We kept our distance. She was cruising so slowly we were even able to move over into other, parallel streets every few blocks—confident that we could pick up her trail again.

In fact we were so engrossed in doing just that— keeping our distance and not arousing her suspicions, that we didn't notice we were gradually moving back closer to the outskirts of our own neighborhood.

Until it was too late!

It was the police car that threw everything and everybody—Lady Thumb and the McGurk Organization alike.

It was parked outside a house—a house that became only too familiar to us as we drew near.

"Machine-Gun Kelly's house!" gasped McGurk.

"Yes—they must be responding to the neighbors' call!" said Brains.

"This late?" said McGurk.

"Probably had to get in touch with the Kellys

first," I said. "Get them to come home and check their belongings."

"Oh gosh! You're right, Joey!" Wanda had slowed to a crawl. "Here comes Mr. Kelly himself!"

The new principal of the Junior High was just emerging from the opening to his driveway. His face looked white, and even at a distance we could tell—from the way he was waving his arms at the patrolman with him—that he was hopping mad.

"We can't go past *there!*" said Wanda.

Nobody argued. Not even McGurk.

"We make a right and go around the other side of the block," he said, already on his way.

Now I did say that *everybody* was thrown by this. Including Lady Thumb. In her case I suppose it was simply the sight of the patrol car, visiting the scene of one of her break-ins earlier than she'd expected.

We didn't realize this, of course, at that moment. We were too busy taking our own evasive action. And I must say she kept her cool much better than we did, because as far as I could tell she maintained her same easy cruising speed as she went past the patrol car.

But at the very next intersection she must have made a turn and—once out of sight of the cop—put her foot down and hightailed it clear out of the area. So we lost her.

"Where'd she *go*?" groaned Willie, after we'd scouted around for maybe fifteen minutes.

"As far from that patrol car as possible," said Mc-Gurk grimly. His frown deepened. "The question we should be asking is this. Where *would* she go?"

"*I've* been thinking about that," said Brains. "My answer is back to base."

"Wherever that *is*," I grunted.

"Well it has to be somewhere around this town," said Brains. "Where she's operating currently. Even if it's only a *temporary* base."

"The camper itself is her *temporary* base, you dummy!" I snapped.

We were all feeling a little sore, I guess.

"Yeah!" said Willie. "She'll just park it anyplace she wants."

It was McGurk who pulled out of this grouchy spin first.

"No, Willie," he said. His eyes were beginning to gleam with their old enthusiastic light again. "Not *anyplace*. There are strict rules about camping out on the streets or in regular parking lots. And someone as clever as Lady Thumb isn't going to get herself busted for some dumb parking violation. No—"

"Trailer sites!" said Brains, lighting up a little himself.

"Right!" said McGurk. "Or wasteland of some kind—away from the houses."

"So we tour the outskirts, McGurk?" said Wanda, mounting up.

"You've said it, Officer Grieg! Come on, men! Get the lead out of your tires. This is now a high-speed search patrol!"

13 Inside the Camper

We spotted her again at exactly 4:25 P.M. EST, that Saturday afternoon.

It *was* on the outskirts, sure enough—in the front parking lot of a burned-down motel on the Old Post Road. It's pretty quiet along there nowadays, with most of the traffic using the new freeway, a few hundred yards farther back. In other words, it was the perfect spot for her to park the camper while operating in our town.

But at first we didn't see the camper. Only Lady Thumb herself, standing at the side of a small Avis rented truck, with her back to the road, bawling out a young man with a close-shaved head and black leather jacket. He looked pretty tough himself, but he wasn't doing much bawling back.

"You dumbbell!" she was yelling. "What d'you want to get a flat for before you've even *started*?"

That was when I noticed the truck had a very heavy list at the back.

"Come on over behind this broken wall, before she notices us," said McGurk.

The wall he meant, a little way behind the truck, was all that was left of one of the motel rooms. And even with this wall and the truck itself between us and the two people, we could hear them plainly.

"*I* couldn't help getting a nail in one of the tires!" The man's voice was rising in protest.

"Sure you could—*idiot*! You could have gone straight from the camper out into the road. But no! You had to show off. You had to drive across all this rubble and stuff, just to raise a cloud of dust, just like a stunt driver in one of those dumb movies you're always watching!"

At the mention of "camper" we all looked around. Then McGurk grunted and pointed along the line of burned-out motel rooms. At the very end, some scrubby bushes had run wild—and through the ragged outline of them we saw the cream top of the camper.

"It isn't as if you had all the time in the world!" Lady Thumb was continuing. "You have to get this stuff over to Newark by six at the latest, and it's four-thirty already!"

"No sweat! I'll—"

"No sweat? *Lots* of sweat, buster! Get busy with that jack. *I'll* fix the spare wheel. Come on. *Move!*"

McGurk made a long hissing sound.

"I bet they have their latest haul in that truck," he whispered. "I bet it's being shipped to a fence. Take its license-plate number, Joey!"

"I already did," I said, showing him my book.

"What now?" whispered Wanda.

"Let's take a look at the camper itself," said McGurk. "They'll be busy on that wheel for another ten minutes at least. Leave the bikes here."

As we made our way, bent double, behind the line of gutted cabins, Brains tried to argue.

"Hey—why don't we go find a phone? Call the cops now? We could have those two caught in possession of stolen property."

"It might take too long," said McGurk. "Besides— we have the truck's number. And besides *that*—we don't know for sure what *is* in the truck. It might be something legal after all."

What he meant, of course, was that he was itching to take a look at the camper and find some direct evidence for himself.

Again we didn't argue. And even Brains began to look excited when we reached the camper and found the double doors at the rear wide open.

"I always did want to see inside one of these things," he said.

Well at first there didn't seem to be much to see. Padded bench seats ran along either side of a small fold-away table. *On* the table was a portable TV set —definitely *not* Mrs. Berg's twenty-four-inch model.

There were shelves above the seats. All I noticed at first were a pile of maps, a cheap suitcase, some cups and saucers. It was Brains who spotted the really incriminating article.

"*There!*" he gasped, pointing to something just out of my angle of vision, behind the suitcase. "That's a tape recorder! The same kind as Mrs. Berg's!"

And with one leap he was inside the camper and examining the recorder more closely.

"Shouldn't we have a search warrant or something?" Wanda murmured doubtfully.

"It is! It is! The very same model and make!" Brains was saying.

That was enough for McGurk—and the rest of us. Without thinking any more about it, we were all inside and crowded around the tape recorder.

Then Willie gave an almighty sniff and turned back toward the doors.

"The toilet—the chemical smell," he said, pointing to a narrow door at the side, in a corner near the main doors.

McGurk stepped across and opened it. There was the toilet, all right—plus a neat little washbasin and more shelves.

"She uses some pretty expensive make-up," said Wanda, staring at the bottles on the shelves.

"Never mind *that!*" said Brains. "How about *this?*"

The space under the washbasin was boxed in. But there was a small door down there, too, partly ajar.

Brains had opened it wider, revealing a can of what smelled like the same chemical even to *my* nose.

But what had really excited him was a metal box at the side of the can. Its lid was wide open, and out of the top jutted a big flashlight, the end of a pair of wirecutters—and the top half of a roll of masking tape.

Green masking tape.

"That's it!" said McGurk. "That's all we need! Now we *can* call the cops!"

But there he was wrong.

Because no sooner had we stepped out of the camper than we heard the roar of an engine. And when we peered through the twigs we saw the truck lurch forward and Lady Thumb begin to march back.

"Quick!" said McGurk. "There's no time to hide. We just have to immobilize the camper and make sure she can't get away. Brains—your knife. Slash a couple of tires while we keep her talking."

But Brains wasn't quick enough. Nowhere near quick enough.

He'd only just managed to get the big blade out of his Swiss army knife, when Lady Thumb came storming around the bushes.

"*Hey! What goes on?*"

Up close, she looked taller and tougher and meaner and more wolflike than ever. She stood with her legs planted firmly apart—long, thin legs in dark jeans—legs that looked as if they could outrun us even on our bikes. Her arms hung loose, but seemed ready to strike like the snake tattooed on the left one, or the lightning bolt on the right. The only softly feminine thing about her was her thin gold necklace—and even that had a razor blade for a pendant. It looked like a *real* razor blade, too!

Anyway, none of us risked trying to make a run for it. McGurk must have made up his mind already to do the exact opposite.

Turning on his most oily grin, he said:

"We—uh—we were just admiring your camper, ma'am."

She flicked him a look, then nodded toward Brains.

"Oh yeah? So why the knife?"

Poor Brains! The blade shook in his hand, under that fierce stare.

"Uh—we—I—*an apple!*" he gasped. "I was going to peel—uh—an apple—ma'am. . . ."

He trailed off and no wonder. The woman didn't even have to speak. Her look of vicious contempt said it for her—"*What* apple?"

And of course Brains had no answer.

By now, McGurk must have figured that there was no chance of stalling our way out. So, with a deep breath, he stepped forward and said:

"All right, lady. We'll level with you. We know what you've been doing. We know about the Four Flying—uh—the garbage kids. And we know how you've been doing the break-ins. We—"

He stopped. The woman's lips had come apart in a kind of silent laugh. It wasn't a very pleasant sight. McGurk took a step back.

But then a change came over her face. The wolf-like ferocity left it, and she became quite normal for a few seconds—even kind of charming.

(*Was this some sort of werewolf woman?* That's what crossed *my* mind at that moment.)

"All right, Red!" she murmured. "How much?"

"M-ma'am?"

"Don't look so stupid. I can see you're as smart as a whip, all of you. How much do you want for keeping your mouths shut?"

McGurk's frown deepened. His chest began to swell up. His face turned red. I thought he was going to *burst* with indignation. After all, this was the second time he was being offered a bribe—*and* in the same afternoon!

"Nothing doing!" he growled.

Lady Thumb's eyebrows shot up.

"Hey, I'm not talking peanuts, you know!" She dug into one of her back pockets. "Here," she said, "how about this? Real gold. Should get you several hundred dollars *at least*."

This time we *all* bristled with indignation.

That wicked woman was holding out a gold pocket watch! She was trying to bribe us with property stolen from a *client*!

The look on our faces must have been enough.

Her own face hardened. Her hands twitched. The snake squirmed. The lightning quivered. Then she relaxed.

"O.K.!" she said, with a sigh. "You win! Go ahead and call the cops."

Wanda, Willie, Brains, and I swung around, already on our way. But McGurk wasn't buying that.

"*Hold it, men!*" He turned to Lady Thumb, and this time his grin had returned in a nonoily form— almost a sneer. "Go call the cops and give you the chance to get away?" He scowled. And again he said it: "Nothing doing!"

The woman shook her head.

"Red! Red! You're one hard man, you know that? O.K.," she said. "Get in the camper. I know when I'm licked. I'd never have gotten far, anyway."

"Huh—get in the camper, ma'am?"

McGurk looked uncertain now.

"Sure!" The woman shrugged. "All of you. I'll take you to police headquarters myself. You can turn me in personally. Why should some dumb cop get credit for the collar when you guys have done all the work? Hop in!"

She had read McGurk exactly right. If she'd schemed for a million years she couldn't have come up with an offer he was less likely to resist.

"Gee! You're a good loser, ma'am, I'll say *that!*" he blurted out boyishly. "And it could make things easier for you when you stand trial," he added, with a look of such terrible adult shrewdness that he nearly went cross-eyed. Then: "Come on, men!" he said. "You heard the lady!"

14 Taken for a Ride

Two things need to be said right away, before any unfriendly person—like Sandra Ennis, for instance, or Burt Rafferty—starts criticizing us for making a dumb, dumb move.

The first thing is that this was the only time we'd ever been given the chance to hand over a real crook to the police. It wasn't exactly an arrest, maybe—and we didn't have our handcuffs with us. But it was the next best thing. So McGurk wasn't the only one of us to be strongly tempted.

The second thing concerns Lady Thumb's manner when she got into the camper. I mean it was so casual, so resigned. She really did act like a good loser, with a sad little smile on her lips. And she didn't even stand over us to make sure we went in first. She left it entirely up to us whether we followed her or not.

When someone in her position gives you every chance in the world to run away, it fazes you. It makes you feel more secure.

It worked like that on us, anyway. And when she didn't even bother to turn her head, as she started the engine—simply saying softly, "All aboard?"—we didn't think twice about saying yes, and closing the doors behind us. Why, we even forgot about our bikes for the time being!

Werewolf? Correction. That woman was more like a *witch*, she was so cunning. It was like we were spellbound just then.

The spell soon began to crack, though. "Oh, excuse me!" said Wanda, remembering. "Our bikes. We left them—" "Tough!" was all Lady Thumb said then, without slowing down. And the spell was completely shattered the moment she turned onto the freeway.

"Hey!" shouted McGurk. "This isn't the way downtown!"

"Tell me about it!" said Lady Thumb, giving a little snigger as she picked up speed.

"Where—where are you taking us?" said Willie.

We'd started by sitting on the bench seats. Now we were standing, crowded behind her.

"I'm taking you for a ride, Beaky!" she said. She glanced in the rear-view mirror as Wanda gasped. "No, don't worry, Wondergirl! Not like in the gangster movies. Just a nice spring Saturday afternoon drive out into the country."

"But you said—" I began.

"What I said, Professor, and what I meant, are two different things."

Her eyes were sparkling in the mirror, but I felt a chill then—believe me. All this giving us special names suddenly seemed very sinister indeed. I remembered reading somewhere that witches use special names for people *when they wish to get them completely in their power*!

"This," said McGurk severely, "is kidnapping. You're only making it worse for yourself, lady."

"Yes," said Brains. "You can get *life* for kidnapping!"

"Little Fuzz! Little Fuzz!" said Lady Thumb reproachfully, eyeing Brains in the mirror. "I'd figured you for being a lot smarter than that. Didn't you hear what I said? I'm not going to hold you prisoner. I'm not going to chop off a finger from each of you and ask your folks for ransom money. No." She passed a slow-moving pickup truck. "All I'm doing is taking you for a ride out into the country. Way out. Miles from anyplace. Then I'm going to stop and let you get out and stretch your legs—nice and civil."

McGurk growled.

"We'll find a phone, don't worry!"

"Ah, yes, Red! But by the time you do, I'll be long gone. Over the state line. . . . So why don't you all settle down and shut up and enjoy the ride?"

"Don't worry!" said Brains, turning to the rest of us. His face was flushed. It had been so ever since she'd renamed him Little Fuzz. He hates to be called Little-anything, and I guess if he'd had his druthers he'd have wanted her to call *him* Professor, not me. "She won't take us far. As soon as she reaches a tollbooth, or stops for traffic lights, we'll jump out!"

"Now that's more like what I expected from you, Little Fuzz," said Lady Thumb. "But I have those bases covered too. One—I'll stick to freeways and country roads—or maybe a parkway *between* toll stations. And two—I'm the best traffic-light judge in the business. I'll make *sure* we reach them on green."

Just to prove it, she slowed down a little as we approached a red in the distance. By the time we'd reached it, it had turned to green.

"Next time she slows down," said Willie, "we'll jump for it *then*."

"What? Out the back door? In traffic? Jumping from a vehicle moving even only at *ten* miles an hour can be fatal. Tell him, Red. Beaky really *is* dumb."

McGurk's face alone would have earned him the name Red, even if his hair hadn't. But his eyes were gleaming.

"She's right, men! There'll be no jumping out at *any* speed. No. I have a better idea."

"What? Just grab her when she slows down?" said Willie, looking very sore—either at being called Beaky, or dumb, or both. "Yeah!"

"NO!" roared McGurk. "You want her to swerve and steer us into a truck?"

"Way to go, Red!" said Lady Thumb. "Now *you* have brains!"

A smirk began to quiver on McGurk's face. But he killed it and scowled.

"Forget her, men! Just move back here. Slide open the windows. You and Wanda that side, Willie. Joey and Brains this side. I'll take the back."

"Then what?" said Wanda.

"We yell and wave and shout for help," said McGurk, beginning to do just that.

Well, we'd reached a section where there was more traffic. It sounded a great idea. Even Lady Thumb seemed to smile with grudging admiration, as she watched us begin to cavort and caper, waving and yelling at other travelers.

I should have known better, though, the moment I saw those witchily twinkling eyes.

Because *she* sure knew better. Lady Thumb knew that if there's one common sight on a freeway on a holiday afternoon, it's a carload of kids fooling around.

So the folks who saw us either waved back, or smiled and shook their heads, even when they were close enough to see our expressions or hear our cries.

"*We're being kidnapped!*" McGurk yelled at a station wagon as it drew level.

This was a big hit.

"So are *we!*" a bunch of kids inside yelled back at us.

So then there were *two* vehicles with frantically waving kids crying kidnap on that freeway.

"You'll yell yourselves too hoarse to make a phone call when I do let you out!" said Lady Thumb, completely unruffled.

By now we could see no houses at all. Just grassy embankments and trees. But there must have been

townships close to the freeway, because Lady
Thumb showed no signs of moving off.

"We have to think of some way of attracting attention while there's still plenty of traffic," muttered
McGurk. "Attracting attention and *holding* it, I
mean."

"I think *I* might know how," I said, already scrib-
bling away. "Brains—you be snipping off four—no—
five strips of that masking tape. About two inches
long."

What I was writing was this—one letter to every page:

That's how we stuck them to the back window, with the strips of tape.

And that's when I saw the first flicker of worry in those eyes in the rear-view mirror.

But—well—you have to face it.

There aren't many *really* sharp-eyed people around. I mean those behind us were either too busy passing to notice, or Lady Thumb herself was too fast in her own passing. Then again there was that same reaction to kids, when people saw us anxiously stabbing our fingers at the sign.

It received two grins in about ten miles, plus one puzzled squint that soon turned into a grin.

However, in those ten miles, another set of brains had started working on the problem. Little F—I mean Officer Bellingham—was big enough to admit later that my idea had given him his.

"It has to be more striking," he said. "More eye-catching. More *unusual*. . . .And I think I know just how."

Already he had the flashlight in his hand.

"Wow!" said Wanda, keeping her voice down, in line with Brains. (It turned out to be *that* good an idea.) "You mean Morse code? In flashes?"

Brains nodded, sending a few practice dots and dashes into the toilet.

"I didn't know you knew the Morse code, Brains," said McGurk.

"Both of them," said Brains.

"*Both* of them?"

"Yep. The Old American and the International. I think I'll use the International. It's better known."

He began to lift the flashlight to the rear window, but McGurk clamped a hand on his shoulder. McGurk's face was glowing so brightly you could almost have passed a hat across it and flashed out a few words of Morse by that method alone!

"Wait!" he said. He glanced around. "This time we have to get folks to realize we're serious," he said. "So—no waving or yelling. In fact keep your heads down. One kid alone flashing for help will look like he means business."

"Yes!" I said, seeing my chance to put the topping

on what, after all, had started out as my idea. "And why don't we *gag* Brains? Just loosely," I added, seeing the look on our science expert's face. "And bind his wrists with masking tape—also loosely. Loosely enough for him to press the switch on and off."

"Joey, I might even start calling you Professor myself!" said McGurk, beaming. "Anyone got a clean handkerchief or something to gag him with?"

Brains had one himself, and inside another minute it was wrapped around his mouth and his wrists were taped and he was flashing his first Morse signal:

· · · ·   ·   ·   —   · ·   ·   —   —   ·

That is the word *help*, if you didn't know it.

Brains told us later that he couldn't resist using a few signals in the American code—the one they used on the old telegraph lines in the U. S. and Canada. *That* version goes like this:

· · · ·   ·   —   · · · ·

Well, we'll never know which did the trick.

In fact at first it looked like neither was any good.

But then, after about fifteen miles, peeking over Brains's shoulder, I saw this old guy driving a 1960 Buick behind us, and I noticed him suddenly stiffen and crane forward over the steering wheel.

Lady Thumb, who'd caught on to what we were doing by now, must have noticed this too. She said nothing—she'd said nothing for most of those fifteen miles, which showed we'd really got her worried this time, I guess. But she did suddenly start accelerating.

When the old guy accelerated with her, still peering at Brains's flashes, I knew we'd made a hit.

But the old Buick was no match for the camper. Lady Thumb, who'd been very careful to keep within the speed limit so far, now put her foot down. Five minutes later, we'd lost the old man.

"Keep going, Brains!" said McGurk. "The guy may be calling the cops right now, but we can't depend on it."

"I umb's gecking *hore!*" protested Brains, through his gag. (Translation: "My thumb's getting *sore!*")

But he did as he was urged.

And then we saw the highway patrol car racing into view behind us, dome light flashing, siren whooping.

15 Trapped

I think McGurk was just a tiny bit disappointed at what happened next. I think he'd have much preferred *four* highway patrol cars to come screaming up—boxing in Lady Thumb in the way he'd had us practice with our bikes.

But one was enough. It very easily pulled level with Lady Thumb. The driver made a waving, pointing movement with his left hand, and Lady Thumb meekly obeyed. She pulled in behind him at the side of the road.

"I didn't know I was traveling that fast, officer," she said, smiling sweetly down on him.

He was tall and lean himself, with a deep tan and

sharp nose. His eyes were sharp, too—sharp and glittery as they ranged over our faces.

"Well now, ma'am," he said, tilting back his hat a little, "there *is* the speeding, too. But—"

"*Too?*" she said, grinning as cool as anything. "What *else* am I supposed to have done?"

"I just had word, ma'am, there's a child on your vehicle, behaving in a strange manner."

"Yes—him!" said McGurk, shoving Brains to the front.

Once again, Lady Thumb's sheer coolness had left us speechless. We'd really expected her to own up immediately, *this* time.

Now that McGurk had broken the silence, however, we all began to speak at once.

McGurk hushed us and pointed to our wizard of the Morse codes.

"Let him speak for himself," he said.

Brains was still struggling with the tape around his wrists. The gag hung loose around his chin.

"I was flashing for help," he said. "In Morse. Both—"

"With that thing tied around your mouth?" said the officer, looking grim now.

All at once I saw what was happening. The fact that Brains's gag and binding were obviously only playacting props made it look like this was still another kids' game.

Lady Thumb saw this too.

"They've been fooling around for *miles*, Officer. Honestly, this is the last time I let kids hitch a ride with *me*!"

"But we *weren't* hitching!" howled McGurk. "We were ab-absconded!"

"Ab*duct*ed," I corrected him. "Taken away against our will."

"I'm beginning to think Red was right first time," said Lady Thumb. "Absconded. Runaways. From some institution for juvenile nuts. Why—" she said, warming up, "*that* one"—she pointed at Brains—"he even held a knife to my throat earlier. 'This is a hijack,' he said. 'Take us to the Canadian border or else!' "

We gasped, growled, yelped—but otherwise we were completely speechless again for a few moments. Stunned by her sheer gall.

"*Do* you have a knife, son?" asked the officer gravely.

"Yes—but—but—" Brains got rid of the last of the tape and pulled out his Swiss army knife. "But it isn't for holding to people's throats!"

It was a funny way of putting it, I know. I guess

in his upset state only the scientific part of Brains's mind was working well, and he was thinking of all the regular uses the knife could be put to. Like opening bottle caps, getting stones out of horses' hooves—that kind of thing.

Oddly enough, it seemed to help our case with the trooper.

He turned to Lady Thumb.

"May I see your driver's license, ma'am?"

"Sure!"

Needless to say, it seemed in order. The only comment the trooper made was to say she was quite a way from Ohio.

"Oh, I know!" she said. "I'm here on a spring vacation, camping around."

"And you?" said the officer, turning to us. "Any identification?"

"Boy, do we have identification!" crowed McGurk. "Show him, men! Show him your ID cards!"

And while the trooper looked at the cards I had made for the Organization (and I swear there was admiration in those glittery eyes) McGurk told him everything we knew about Lady Thumb.

"What an imagination!" she said, rolling up her eyes. "I'll say this for you, Red—you—"

"The watch in her back pocket isn't imagination!"

said Wanda. "Make her show it to you, sir. Then read what it says on the back."

Lady Thumb didn't turn a hair.

"Sure," she said. "Take a look, Officer. A gift from my poor old Uncle Walt. A—a bequest, really. After he died."

And she made her eyes flutter like they were going to shed tears.

The trooper examined the inscription, but of course her mention of "Uncle Walt" made it seem to check out.

I frowned. There had to be *something*—something to settle this argument, but I couldn't quite think what!

Then I remembered my notebook.

"Here, sir!" I yelled, flipping to the page about Mrs. Berg's break-in. "How come we knew the details of that inscription? Word for word!"

Again Lady Thumb had an answer.

"Because you must have copied it down. When I passed the watch around for you to admire . . . ." She fluttered her eyelashes at the trooper. "*Anything* to quiet them down, Officer. They were behaving so rowdily at that point."

But Trooper Gould (we found out his name later) was no fool.

Something else on that page had caught his eye. He looked up at the shelf behind us.

"Tell me something, ma'am. Is that tape recorder your own?"

She blinked. Then shrugged.

"Sure. I bought it only a few days ago. Store in Manhattan."

"Then you'll know what is on the tapes?" said the trooper, mildly.

"Well—uh—sort of. I haven't had time to listen to them much, yet."

"No. But the *kind* of thing?"

Her eyes were blinking rapidly now. I could almost hear her brain clicking over—trying to remember what Mrs. Berg's place was like, then trying to imagine the owner's likely taste in music.

"Oh—just sort of easy-listening stuff," she said. "Sweet and low—that kind of thing."

It was a good try.

But not good enough.

"Son," the trooper said to Brains, who was nearest the shelf. "Would you mind turning it on?"

"Sure thing!" said Brains, pressing switches already.

And then, into that camper on that sunny spring afternoon, came one of the eeriest sounds I ever heard.

First, the hiss of a tape. Then a harsher hissing, like somebody's asthmatic breathing. Then a dull distant tapping.

Then the main sounds. A wheezing, grunting, squawling, horrible noise, like a wounded animal, punctuated with grunts and muttered "Darns!" Then it picked up and the tune became vaguely recognizable.

"Easy-listening stuff, huh?" said the trooper, fingering his gun butt. "Sweet and low stuff, huh? O.K., son," he said to Brains. "Switch it off before it gives me an earache. I'm no musician, but I can recognize *Turkey in the Straw* when I hear it. Even when it's played like *that!*"

"But—I—I haven't really played that tape before. I'd no idea—"

"So you didn't play it this afternoon at all, while the kids were with you?"

"Er—no—I—"

"So how come this kid here has it all down in his notebook? . . . Lady—I'm going to have to take you in for questioning. Just put your left hand through the steering wheel and hold the other outside of it, please."

She did this, glaring at him and us while he snapped on the handcuffs.

We cheered.

Then he took the key out of the ignition, turned to us and said:

"I'm going to call in for reinforcements. A lady officer to frisk our friend here—"

"Wanda's a lady officer!" said McGurk, eagerly, but the man shook his head and continued:

"This has to be done correctly. Also I'll need another two officers—one to drive the camper in, and

one to drive the lady officer and our prisoner here
back. *You* guys can ride with me."

He chuckled as we walked over to his car.

"Only no flashing help messages from the back
of *my* wagon, O.K.?"

Then, just before he reached for the microphone
to call in, he said something I shall remember with
pride all my life.

"Young fella," he said, "you keep one heck of a
good notebook there. You know that?"

Which was where McGurk had to chip in.

Naturally!

"Sure, Officer!" he said. "I trained him well. I
train *all* my staff well."

16 One Very Special Loose End

And that was that. End of case. We still hadn't been able to make our personal arrest, of course, but our visit to the Highway Patrol station that afternoon was a very satisfying one.

Because Lady Thumb didn't attempt to tell any more lies after that. How could she, with my notebook and all the evidence we'd amassed?

Besides, even while we were on our way to the station, a vital message was being received there.

"Looks like the kids' story of a rented truck checks out, Billy" one of the officers said to Trooper Gould. "Some guy got himself busted for speeding in one. On the Cross Bronx Expressway. About a half-hour ago. Couldn't account properly for the stuff in back.

Tried to make a break for it. He's spilling his guts to the Westchester boys. You say something, lady?"

We were in the vestibule, and she was just being led in by the lady officer. She'd overheard what the man had said (because he'd wanted her to, I figure!). But although her eyes clouded and her shoulders slumped, she didn't crack entirely. All she said was, "*That* dumb ape!"

Then she turned to McGurk and, with a sudden dazzling—yes, *bewitching* smile, she said:

"Now that's something *you'd* never do, Red! If only you'd been older"—she sighed—"what a team we'd have made!"

His first reaction was disgust. I thought he was going to throw up on the spot as they led her away.

But over the next few days he began to get a dreamy look in his eyes whenever her name was mentioned.

"You have to hand it to her," he kept murmuring. "Lady Thumb was the worthiest opponent I—we ever had."

Witchcraft again! Even at a distance.

But you know how I broke the spell?

At the end of the notice on our door, McGurk had tacked on the latest addition:

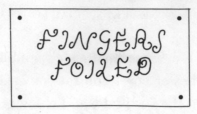

FINGERS
FOILED

And after a while, I realized this was incomplete.
Also I remembered that witches can work their
spells through gaps like that.

So *I* wrote out another addition and tacked *that*
on. And ever since then he's lost the dreamy look
when the woman's name is mentioned.

What *was* it I wrote, to seal it off properly?
This:

THUMBS THWARTED!
†   †